Autumn

Robert W. Williams

Autumn
Written by Robert W. Williams
Copyright 2011 ©
On file with the Library of Congress – All rights reserved
Find information and other titles at:
RobertWWilliamsAuthor.com

B.W.I.P., LLC.
225 State Street
Enola, PA 17025

First Edition February/2011

Edited by Mark 'Mel' Matheson

ISBN # 1456560131

Other titles by Robert W. Williams:

Antigravity: The Novel
Song of the Seventh Angel

Photo by Lisa Siciliano - Dogdazephoto.com

Acknowledgements

I would like to thank all the women I have ever spoken with that have shared their thoughts about love and marriage candidly, without whom; I would not be able to write with both a listening ear and a speaking voice toward the heart of a female character, or reader.

I would like to especially thank my good friend Kim Martin for helping me through the toughest of times regarding the completion of this story. I would also like to thank Lydia Zavala for showing me the true meaning of friendship, and for helping to restore my faith in God.

Thank you…

…and to Cynthia Abbott, for teaching me that a dream has not come true until you can hold it in your hand.

This story is dedicated to a very beautiful young woman by the name of Joy Sanderson, and to all the many wonderful characters in my life, both real and imagined.

Autumn creeps up slowly, winding its way through the dry and brittle cornstalks within the fields of late August like a shimmering yet transparent serpent made of uneasiness and wind. Cooling the mornings, lowering the sunsets toward the horizon, darkening the shadows beneath streetlamps; autumn wraps the world in cashmere and wool with its promises of fireside comforts, as opposed to the sultry silks of summer and springtime's cottony wears.

Autumn creeps up slowly, more slowly than the freckled green of a pumpkin's shell can fade to sunset orange over the course of many nights. Autumn, at times, is brisk and dull, a misty shade of foggy white within the morning. Autumn can be crisp like a cucumber and brightly lighted. Autumn is the mother of softer sunrays than is summer. Autumn persuades the eggs to emerge from the white moth's succulent abdomen so she may hide her future presents beneath the coming snow. Autumn prepares us for the future. Autumn mystifies and chills even the sharpest of our minds.

Autumn calls upon the bats of night to swirl within pre-slumber twilight blues so they might feast beneath the stars upon all things that might annoy.

Autumn causes us to take pause; to wonder what might lie beyond the end of that twisting, turning road.

Autumn shows us just how many of life's changes are far from permanent, and autumn proves to us that deep green lawns can hibernate more perfectly than any bear or woodland mouse.

Autumn is frightening. *Autumn scares.*

Autumn narrates the precious development of the delicate yet resilient human soul while tempering our resources to honest perfection beneath our skin.

Autumn perpetuates the myth that eternal love may be a dying sentiment, teasing you and teasing me – strumming us - even plucking away at our heartstrings with each of its falling leaves while allowing us to realize that spring is not the only season in which one might truly fall.

Autumn is a time of mass seeding and mass sowings, whereas the lesser observant still perceive that time of year as

1

being the sole vocation of spring.

Autumn forces us to attempt to reason with our mortality as if it possessed a brain.

Autumn bears the weight of all our fears, with its scent, bold and pungent, familiar, bearing a striking resemblance to a mixture of crushed, dried flowers, soil, the decay of adolescence, and tears. Autumn is a potpourri of lamentation and of heartache, sadness, even longing; it is a planter full of coleus vying for attention from a dark and dusty corner by the garage.

Autumn is the spider web's last and only friend.

She entered the gathering in a low-cut blouse whose pattern and coloration spoke effusively of nothing less enticing than a tequila infused sunset dappled with patches of green. I smiled at her comeliness, an image I knew all too well from having seen her before. In fact, I had been hoping I would see her there that very evening.

I said, "I haven't seen anything so intriguing as your blouse since the last time I had the pleasure to see Jerry Garcia and the boys at an outdoor session last June."

She smiled back, wide eyed with interest, excitedly replying with, "Have you? I mean, seriously, have you really?"

Her eyes were sparkling like dewdrops, becoming then as onyx spheres having received a generous anointing of oil. She was younger than I and this was quite evident.

"Have you?" she pressed, "I mean, if you don't mind me asking, have you really experienced that sort of thing? A hippy show? Was it a *love-in*?" She said this last remark in nearly a whisper, looking over her shoulders to see if anyone else could hear.

I think I may have even blushed then. I had always wanted to meet her.

"Oh!" and she was wriggling as a child might, imploringly, and I could see that she could sense that my answer would have to be yes. "Please tell. Was it wonderful? I've heard so many stories, good and bad." She looked around again, "Was it inspiring? Was it everything they say it is? Was it the most beautiful thing you have ever experienced?"

2

"Not so much as you…" was all that I could think then.

* * * * *

Autumn is the sound of millions upon millions of leaves cheering for the acts of the Almighty from the grandstands of the world.

* * * * *

I answered her in the only appropriate manner in which I could at such a gathering, "Yes. And it was inspiring. In fact, it was the second most beautiful thing I have ever experienced."

Third. I guess I lied.

Her tender eye-light flickering in the soft amber glow of the party, she continued to ask me questions like an innocent. We did not even know one another's names.

She changed her tone as if on cue, as if I had already let her down by hesitating. "Oh really," she asked, "and what was the first most beautiful thing?" and her eyes were delicately dissecting mine, inspecting me for flaws, for pleasantries, and for clues, "Please, I have to hear this. I am so curious, you would not believe."

"The first most beautiful thing I have ever experienced?"

"Yes." She was rubbing her knees together like a cricket engulfed in the warmth of anticipation.

"Well, that would have to be forgiveness." I put my wine glass down on the table. "Being forgiven is definitely the most beautiful thing I ever experienced in my life. Especially when I really, really needed it and felt for sure I did not deserve it."

Her only response was to emit a soft, warm sigh of instant relief.

* * * * *

Autumn provides us with the most delicious aspects of feeling both pleasantly worn out and tired while also feeling comfortably alert and aware, even refreshed. It wraps security around stimulus, re-awakens us to the fact that we shall all pass away some day, and it delivers this sentiment kindly, and calmly, with little fanfare aside from the changing of leaves.

With leaves of every shade and color, save for blue, autumn speaks to us of subtlety within the spectrum of existence, of being bold without pretense. Autumn speaks of forgetfulness, of cinnamon, of wanderlust and apples, of laziness and mountain streams, nutmeg, and the low hum of ten trillion dying bees.

Late August whispers tales from mason jars packed with fruit preserves, and buckets and buckets of wild honey, while September sings to us its cherished songs of golden mead.

She looked so beautiful that day, August 28th, 1973.

The hallowed Moon of late August is a Holy symbol and a servant to humankind. The harvest Moon that follows is a harbinger of dark and chilly things to come.

*   *   *   *   *

The first days of September can bring us close to walking the proverbial plank of fear and desolation. Its solitude can leave us sitting on the couch wondering what it was we were just about to do.

Autumn is a time for recollective sleeping, for weeping tears for heaven and for weeping tears of heavenly joy. A time for watching as our children grow, for listening; for learning to strengthen ourselves, and for strengthening each other so that we may face the future on our own. It is a time to read. It is a time for saying goodnight to early dawns and for welcoming the morning with loving hugs and warmer mugs. Sometimes alone, quite often together, autumn is the perfect time of year to turn to God.

*   *   *   *   *

Autumn is the eleventh hour of the dreamer. Autumn feels like care, yet it smells like firewood and freshly washed hair.

4

Autumn, although a word, has no specific location, so it really isn't there...

* * * * *

She was still smiling; this lone, Christian beauty, a woman I had seen before at church, a woman I had always hoped to meet. I was quite convinced she was still curious, if not merely being polite. I returned her pleasantly inviting gesture and waited for her to ask what it was she had been dying to ask me all along.

"Did you see God?"

I picked up my wine glass and a cracker.

"People have told me," she whispered, "and I have read articles, many articles in magazines where people claim you see God during the experience. Is it true?"

* * * * *

Autumn is the perfect time to think again...

* * * * *

Twenty years ago I may have said yes to that question, that is, if it had been anyone else but she that had asked the question.

Back then, we all thought we were 'seeing God' when we experimented with mind altering, mind expanding, and perception enhancing chemicals and plants. Now, in hindsight, I know we were not *seeing God*; it was just another take on things, another point of view.

A year before I met Susan, well, I might have said yes then too. However, what I have learned since then is that, when God chooses to reveal Himself, you do not need drugs to discover Him.

God is always there, but you cannot see Him... because God is perfectly clear.

So I answered her the only way I knew how, "No. I have never seen God. No one ever has, but I do see His fingerprints and His signature all over creation. I hear His voice whenever I listen. I feel His love, and I do see the glory in His power and presence everywhere and in everything. I see His movements and His motions, His affect upon everything in the universe and everything I do. But no, drugs won't get you any closer to God unless you O.D."

She was glistening. Her teeth were sparkling. Her eyes were pure blossoms of starlight caged like fireflies within two perfect spheres.

I saw no reason to stop talking.

"And I see by the look in your soul, as I gaze through your windows, young lady," and I winked to let her know that I was referring to her eyes, "that you are no stranger to the love and forgiveness of our Lord, and not merely here for the food and the wine."

She pursed her lips then as her head began to nod forward.

I still did not know her name.

* * * * *

Autumn is a turnstile in the passage toward the holidays for many, yet for so many others, autumn is simply a pause.

Autumn is an unwrapped gift box awaiting the presence of patience, then the impatience of nimble fingers as they paw.

Autumn *is* a just reward for all the faithful.

Autumn's exchange with us is like free, outdoor air conditioning for the weary. It is a tall cool drink of water at the end of a long, very hot and very difficult day.

Autumn is the answer to the prayer that summer prays as she wipes the waxy sweat from her dry, bruised, soiled, and ill-sutured brow as she continues straining. Autumn is the elixir that can stave the ills of spiritual dehydration. Autumn is a natural remedy.

I never really knew what it was about her. Perhaps it was the

6

way she admired me when she first walked into the building; that sort of complimentary flattery best achieved with the eyes and the way in which someone walks toward you. Perhaps that was the first thing that struck me; how she looked to me with such surprise, such innocent surprise within her countenance, as if she had been anticipating our meeting for ages, but had not yet known it would be me.

Perhaps God had created this suspense by keeping us apart until that particular evening, until that moment on that night.

It could have also been that other look in her eyes...

This young woman wore a look that told me she was desperately in need of rescuing, so terribly in need of something tangible and true onto which she could hold that it was eating her alive inside. She looked as if she was sizing me up as a potential candidate despite the fact that I had been retired from the half-life of rescuing wayward women for some time. Perhaps it was our mutual love for our Savior and our utter admiration for, and our deeply shared reverence for God?

I still do not know to this day... yet I do, perhaps I do. From my perspective, I sum all of it up as her beauty, but her personal perspective I may never fully know.

I never asked her. I only received bits and pieces over time.

* * * * *

Autumn is the crackle deep within the burning twig.

* * * * *

Her eyes were twinkling. The possessiveness expressed by her presence made me think back to Solomon's words from The Book of Proverbs. She shook me up all over, and she frightened me a little with her intensity, yet I was compelled to stay and hear more.

She seemed to brighten as she neared me, yet the lighting in the room had not changed at all, at least not discernibly or by the switching of any electrical power by any human hand.

7

How could it have been so?

How could I have fallen so deeply in love or lust with this woman so quickly? Was she the image of my teacher, that crush I had in Junior High? Was she the combined image of all my first crushes from grade school through High School? I will never truly know.

Everything, even down to the curls, her flare, her teeth, her smile - her zest for all things wonderful - and I could tell these things even before she first spoke to me. Her eyes were the eyes of every woman I had ever wanted, every woman I had ever fallen in love with. Those magnificent and wonderful blue eyes…

How could it have been so, that she could have been all these women, all these incredible memories and living essences, and all this, without even trying?

Was it all for me? I seriously wondered if God had created this woman for me, had now even delivered her to me. I could have called her Eve then…

How could she be so?

How could it be so, that I, this barely audible whisper of a freshly saved man, a sinner who had been longing for the company of a saved woman for what seemed like forever; for her, for the one… How so, I asked myself, how could she suddenly appear in my life, to fill my eyes with wonder, and instantly fill my heart with so much, with so much, and all at once.

And that's when I noticed her ring.

* * * * *

Autumn is the principality of vagueness and ambiguity, although, as seasons go; autumn is very precise with her predictions.

* * * * *

The ring she wore was not anything to write home about, in fact, it was pretty much plain. However, in the truest of simplistic and golden abstractions in circular form, it was unmistakably a wedding band, and that meant something.

In fact, it meant everything to me. For a moment, I wondered just how much it meant to her...

*   *   *   *   *

Autumn is sincere in her subtlety. She is acutely aware, yet as vague as the memory of a dream half-enjoyed upon awakening in early morn. She is as ambiguous as a hint from a loved one who wants something from you, yet autumn is always willing to give you something in return. Her colors are blindingly bold at times, yet softened by the distance, sparingly, and she does this all as if by some whisper within ease beyond suspicion as she compares. She is also overtaking and provocative, as if nature itself has something to hide, alluringly willing to reveal all these things and more as time passes. This thing, all these things are something we must discover for ourselves as we explore.

Autumn wears the lingerie of every year.

*   *   *   *   *

September days are woven from the wispy, fluttery strands of the weeping willow and the cottony tufts of milkweeds puffs combined with cottonwood. They are blending with the near silence of their callings as they float and drift within the breeze. September days are something.

September days might as well go by unnumbered.

An afternoon in September is a gift you can share with a friend: A mug of Chai tea with cream, perhaps a sweater, or even a long and casual walk along the avenue at the end of a busy day. The gift of a walk along the avenue just to gaze at all the colored leaves as time goes by unfettered, without distraction or any rules. Time is a gift that needs no receipt.

*   *   *   *   *

She had heard about me from some of the others. I later discovered this bit of information while staring at her ring; oblivious to any of the other current thoughts she may have been expressing. For a moment, I was wishing that her ring was not what it appeared to be. I was hoping it was a promise ring; the type many of the young virgins wear as a promise to remain pure until marriage, but it was not. In a last ditch attempt to thwart reality, I was hoping it was a fake ring, a rouse designed to keep all the hungrier, more aggressive men at bay. A deterrent, an illusion she wore like a necklace of garlic one might wear in the countryside woods of Transylvania. I was hoping she would turn out to be single, unattached, and unafraid.

Though I begged of this from Heaven, this would not turn out to be.

* * * * *

When September arrives, summer slowly closes the door on August gatherings. Her swimming pools, her vast parades of endless fire trucks and little children, veterans and the pretty girls with their twirling batons and their red, white, and blue caped leotards. Her picnic tables put away, along with her tablecloths and many colored balloons; September shuts the door on a month that starts with a delicate vowel, cramming her vacation photos into wooden boxes in the attic for many years to come.

September closes the door to summer like Susan's gold clad finger nearly closed my heart to the promise of love.

How was I ever going to know her?

How was I ever going to be her friend without falling in love with her and wanting to have her? How could I go on forever without ever knowing this young woman's touch? How was I ever going to be that strong?

I wondered. I truly did.

* * * * *

Autumn is one of the many prices we pay for the gift of having once been small children. It is a time for those who dye their grays to reckon with the truth that we are all getting older, and that gray in turn becomes silver, and that silver hair and hay straw are part of autumn's precious ways.

Sensing that she was everything I had ever wanted to meet in a woman; honest, sparkly, effervescent, intelligent, energetic, happy, sensitive, bubbly, content, enlightening, inspiring... endlessly inspiring. These things I had always looked for in a woman, yet I had not found them all until I met Susan.

I knew I had to do something desperate, and I knew I had to do it quickly if I was to get away. I took my eyes off her ring at once and looked deeply into her eyes then.

My eyes met, at first, with the warm reception of her near perfect smile.

My desperation led me to the only conclusion I would ever find: I knew then, right then, because I could not leave her; that I would have to learn to love this woman respectfully, even promisingly, swearing platonically for the rest of my natural life...

As a friend.

* * * * *

Autumn crushes fox grapes into winter's jellies, mixes stream water with dusty old turkey feathers, gobbling up the morning dew.

The second day of September is a hearty commitment. The day you first begin to realize that October is really on its way. It is the day you first appreciate and understand that the skin tightening, or loosening, on the vein covered back of your hand is forcing you to acknowledge the fact that you; yes you, are growing older.

Some refer to the first days of September as "back to school."

* * * * *

So I told myself I could never run and that I had to know this woman. It was inevitable; any other option would have been unsuitable, even unacceptable to me. I told myself there was no possibility that I could walk away without knowing her beautifully, and I told myself I would love both her *and* her husband as one.

Either way I vowed to myself, and to God, that I would never so much as touch Susan's hand unless her marriage ended in a divorce... or with his death.

Sometime later, I would have to admit all of this to her.

* * * * *

The feel of September is like the feeling we get when hugging the softest of pillows, whereas August is like rolling around in deep, warm sand.

Autumn is a besting of confidences.

Autumn is a woman and a man.

Autumn is the harvest – when death dances merrily beneath the mighty oak, where wheat dries, where cocoons blend within the sweet detritus – a hiding place for the howls of the unsaved, where the lost... where we *all* must reap the bitterness of evil seeds that we have sown.

September days remind us all to stop, to halt, to turn around before moving forward in order to recollect where it is that we have been. To understand what it is we have received, and what we have seen; to acknowledge all the reasons why we have done the things we do.

September days are days of choosing. September is the month of the great, wooden fork in the road. The piper, polishing his flute, this stringer of the harp unstrung, casts a knowing smile before he plays his final tune for us all to follow to the shores before we all must board that boat and say farewell. Southbound geese and airplanes, all leave you behind alone to choose... What will you do?

Autumn is a time of daring, a time for sweet remembrance over lemon, toast, and tea.

A Sunday morning in September can often pry the misery

from our souls like a sewer cap lifted from the surface of the street in order to shed light on what lies beneath the surface. A Saturday in September can remind you of the day you were born.

It had only been five minutes or so since we had first stood eye to eye in the gathering. I was the taller, she, more delicate, smaller, petite, and yet her soul could have reached to the sky. Her eyebrows, which remained almost in their natural condition, spoke volumes of her nature, and the kindness and compassion she would eventually prove to display.

* * * * *

It is strange how we, as human beings, confuse our love, so often, with passing infatuation. I, for one, fall into states of compelling infatuation almost daily. I feel blessed that way, but even more so blessed by a newfound ability to know the difference every time.

Discernment is a wonderful gift.

I will admit now to how immediately struck by Susan's presence I truly was that evening, and how I did not hesitate to allow myself to fall for her, assuming I could have even tried to avoid those feelings at all. Smitten, bowled over, sullied by her contagious yet casual sensuality; I was taken. Yet, in time she would teach me of a greater love – a love independent of sexual trappings – a respectful love, and it all began at once when I saw that golden ring.

* * * * *

Autumn is an oyster being shy about its pearl.

* * * * *

Peculiar enough was the fact that we began our life-long love, our particular relationship, with a reference, or should I say an inquiry into my experiences with the hallucinogenic substances I'd ingested at a rock concert. Even still her choice of blouse, and how that pretty blouse had caught my eye, but even more so beguiling to me was the fact that she had come to the gathering alone, sans husband, only to meet me, with me in mind.

Susan would later admit to me, even that very evening, how she had worn that blouse with the hope of attracting the eyes, but not the lust, of someone as colorful, and she used these words, *as adorable* as me.

It was what she felt she needed. Her desire, and her intention, was to establish a Godly friendship with a man, specifically me, in the hopes of better understanding her husband and his ways.

"Then I think it would be more appropriate," I said sternly, holding onto what may have been unsubstantiated ground, "and furthermore, more greatly beneficial to you and healthier *for* you, to develop such a friendship with your husband, so that in knowing him more closely as a friend, you could better understand him and his ways." I said this with fortitude and much belief in my own words.

Her eyes welled up with tears that would not fall just then. Her tears simply filled her eyes to the brim and then crest but ceased to swell beyond the breaching point of her lower eyelids. Mesmerized by her sudden display of emotion as she candidly revealed her suffering to me, all her pain as it rose to the surface; she then shattered me with these eight impossible words:

"I can't. He will not talk to me."

* * * * *

Summer is the well worn ungula of spring digging awkwardly and hungrily, even soulfully into the dry and barren soil of our common disbelief.

* * * * *

A lesser man, perhaps a weaker man, even me some months before, would have offered her another drink and moved in for

14

the kill.

I did not. I simply listened, and in turn, I chose to offer some semi-spiritual reply.

* * * * *

Autumn is a time of burning flowers.

* * * * *

Instead of trying to take advantage of her, I told her that God loves her very much. Then I reminded her that she had chosen to marry this man; that he was her choice. Then I did my best to explain to her that I could in no way rescue her from her dilemma, but that I could offer her my advice.

I still did not know her name at this point as we had failed to make, or had skipped our introductions.

"Whatever it is you want to say to me, say to him. Open his heart. It is not his reluctance to speak with you that is hindering the growth of your relationship, but perhaps it is the fact that you are approaching him as your husband, and not as a friend. Could it be that the fear of being open, brave, and honest with him is really what is getting in the way?"

Her tears began to fall just then. The levy had finally broken. Her tears flowed heavily from each of her crystal blue eyes.

Then I too, deep inside, although not visibly, began to hurt tremendously, and not only for her, but also for me.

* * * * *

Autumn is to the seasons as lovely music is to a funeral. Autumn soothes, although many are reluctant to embrace its healing powers. Autumn caresses, autumn enlivens, so please remove yourself to the outdoors. Autumn blesses, and nothing will ever compare to this eternal harvest of life until you reach God's Heaven above.

Autumn is the wheat field of your soul.

* * * * *

Autumn brings about the red and yellow sumac. Autumnal waters pull the poc-poc and the slap-slap from the rivers' sloshing shores. Autumn lulls the boats to sleep.

Autumn plays for keeps.

* * * * *

"So, how long have the two of you been married?" I asked with my voice slightly cracking, not too drastically interested in hearing the answer at all.

* * * * *

Autumn is a time for generous and unbridled laughter, the sort of laughter we share when we finally come to the realization that we are all tremendously in favor of no longer feeling alone.

* * * * *

Honestly, I detested the question. I loathed the question and I loathed asking her that question. The only answer I wanted to hear was that their divorce was pending or that the ink was already drying on the papers after all concerned parties had signed.

I know it is selfish and evil, and I know it was wrong to be thinking such things, but one cannot control his mind in a weakened condition, he can only control his actions. The truth is, Susan was everything I had ever wanted to find in a woman, except that she was no longer single of course, and as long as I am being honest, she could have afforded to gain a few pounds. Sure, it is a crude sentiment, but I like a little meat on a women.

"We've been married for a little over a year," she said with a languishing pause. "Our wedding was last June. Last, last June."

16

She was not quite finished wiping her tears away then.

"It wasn't like this at the beginning. I mean, I had my eyes open – he did everything right – but it all changed after we said our vows."

That was the first lie Susan ever told to me, although, at the time, she had no idea she was lying. My point is that nothing had changed other than the fact that, once married; Susan had finally opened her eyes. That is what happens when you pay more attention to the wedding than you are willing to pay to the eventuality of a marriage when you think you have fallen in love.

* * * * *

Autumn is about honestly facing the facts.

* * * * *

She told me, "To me, life is like hiking up a mountain path while stopping along the way to fill up your backpack with stones. The mountain path is the path that leads to your happiness, and each stone represents an act of negativity, evil, or sin. Eventually, we find it harder and harder to climb with this weight bearing down upon us, affecting us, weight that might otherwise never go away. Opening your heart to Christ empties the backpack, leaving you free to climb, and to help others."

It was a case of near full-disclosure with Susan right from the start. I found out more about another's spiritual perspectives and about another couple's marriage than I ever cared to learn in the first fifteen minutes that I knew her. I listened, because for some reason, even beyond Christian Brother and Sisterhood, I felt I really cared about her troubles and for her.

We stood together in the rain, sharing a cigarette, and she blessed me right there by letting me know I was not creepy, and that she knew in her heart she could trust me, alone.

"A lot of men are creepy, you know. You can feel what their

eyes are doing and you can actually hear their true intent in their sentences… in all of their words. But you're not like that. I don't feel any of that with you."

"Thank you." I said as if I was cowering inside.

Susan exhaled deeply and said with a simple laugh and with a smile as we stood out in the rain, "No. Thank you, and I mean that."

* * * * *

Autumn is the feeling the entire room experiences the moment the birthday candles are blown out.

* * * * *

"You really need to be more careful with how much you are willing to say, right away." I said this to her.

"Why?"

"Well, it's full-disclosure; you open yourself up to being vulnerable and, in exposing yourself, you can end up feeling unstable or insecure because too many people whom you may not fully trust know all of your problems. For some; it is the root of paranoia, for others it simply opens them up to harm and anxiety."

"But I trust you. The Holy Spirit told me I could trust you as soon as I saw you."

I was not going to deny her that.

She followed with, "The last thing I am going to do is doubt that. I wish I had listened to the Holy Spirit before I…"

I could not argue with her reasoning. She had me stymied. She was going to say, "Before I said, "I do.""

She abruptly changed the subject though, "Oh, what I was saying is that he, my husband, believes a woman's work is women's work and that a man's world is outside the home. When he comes home from work he wants to treat me like a…"

She would not say the word.

"He wants to order me around, and I hate it. Worst of all, it is just so damn hypocritical on his part that it kills me."

She was hogging the cigarette, so I rolled and lit a second. She did not notice.

"How's that?" I asked just out of curiosity.

"He's hypocritical because my husband is a black man."

* * * * *

Autumn is the crow's last chance for a nice, warm roadside meal beneath the Sun.

* * * * *

I want to tell you now that I fought hard to resist temptation. As I had been pigeon holed into the role of "Nice guy" by this beautiful, married, young woman, a depiction I wanted to live up to ever since the moment I accepted the Lord; I felt in one sense relieved. However, as she revealed more and more to me concerning her husband's lack of consideration toward her, I began to feel my heartstrings being pulled. I began to feel my testosterone levels rising. I could feel a sympathetic and powerful passion begin to possess me, and deep inside I simultaneously prayed for the strength to resist her, and admittedly prayed that her story would conclude in a want for divorce.

* * * * *

Autumn is the season of some of our toughest family choices.

* * * * *

"I love my husband, don't get me wrong, and I don't want to divorce him… I just want…"

Her eyes, at the same time adoring my trustworthiness, were also imploring me to say the words she could not say aloud.

Then I said them.

"You just want to change him into the kind of man you would have married if you had only been more patient," and that is when this yet-to-be-named young, married woman really began to cry, although, for the record, each of her tears fell in undisturbed silence.

* * * * *

Autumn is the season of kindergarten weepings; when children separate from their mothers and fathers, and parents walk away, or drive away, shedding tears of unprecedented heartache they never knew could have ever possibly existed anywhere inside of them before. A child's tears might end as soon as they enter the classroom. A mother's tears might last that entire first day of school.

* * * * *

Susan turned away from me so she could cry her tears alone. She did not walk away from me; she just turned her head away. That was the very first time she ever hurt me, but I guess I had earned every ounce of that pain.

* * * * *

Autumn gets people to open up their cookbooks, to blow the dust off their mixers, their cutting boards, and bowls. The first week of September gets people to call up older relatives to ask for that favorite family recipe, that special something or other they remember from the past.

In September, we begin to notice change as holiday decorations start filling up the store shelves. We think of mortgages, about possibly trading in those old ski boots and replacing all those cracked and faded plastic jack-o-lanterns of the fall.

Autumn reminds us of those who have passed on before us, and how we might never find those recipes again.

* * * * *

Susan did not have to try to look beautiful. She was beauty embodied in my humble opinion. Maybe not in the eye of every beholder, but to me she was more than physically attractive. She was electrifyingly unique. She was alive with something special and it showed.

Susan was a source of positive energy that could have ultimately spun a thousand windmills, she could have spun straw into gold, powered photovoltaic cells and illuminated light bulbs; she could have ignited a thousand furnaces just by walking by. She could have aided plants in the process of photosynthesis. She could have been a source of heat for a group of survivors trapped in the bitter snow.

This one young woman could have put a manic swing on a bi-polar experiencing depression. She could have tricked an autumn day into believing it was spring.

* * * * *

Autumn is the time of year we really begin to understand how much our children have grown. All God's children, that is.

* * * * *

Susan was a firefly of many colors: A blue-eyed lightning bug with a cute and shapely behind. She was a curly, golden haired glowworm, and slender, and pretty at that.

She had curly hair with rivulets of sable-soft brown… and forest gold.

* * * * *

Autumn is an apple. Take a bite from the Indian summer and close your eyes while lying down.

* * * * *

On top of that, Susan was a true and faithful believer, and at that time and even after, this quality of hers was the most important thing to such a man as me.

* * * * *

I could hardly believe I was talking with her. I could hardly believe she was there. At first, I had a difficult time deciding whether I was entertaining an angel, which she was, or may have been, in a way. I found it difficult not to stare.

I had turned twenty-nine that spring. I had been single all my life. Sure, I had a few girlfriends, and one or two I even thought I might eventually marry, but each time I realized how that individual would surely remain the same; I had to walk away from the possibility of engagement. Why? Because people rarely change and I did not want to end up like Susan. None of the woman I had ever dated ever felt like home to me.

Susan said, "It was different before we got married and now I seriously wonder if I had been manipulated. At first, he said all the right things, and he even attended church with me once or twice. But as soon as we got married, all he wanted to do was to hang out with all of his friends until he was ready for me to serve him dinner… or to provide him with s-e-x."

She actually took the time to spell out the word.

* * * * *

The chill in the air in autumn, placed there by God to wake us all up like some sort of spiritual alarm clock, is something many of us never come to understand, or appreciate. It is spiritual smelling salts, designed to aid both the faint of heart and the terminally unaware, which most of us are.

Love can be blind, they say, and autumn's chill, placed cyclically within eternity, is there to open our eyes.

* * * * *

"Before we got married, we never really ate dinner together

unless it was pizza or a burger. One of the reasons I could not wait for us to settle down, and to get married, was for all of that to end. I kept imagining that we would be cooking together and eating meals together all of the time. I pictured him coming home and chopping onions while I shaped a pie." She rolled her eyes, "Now all he does is come home from work, hang out with his friends, or go to the bar until dinnertime, and then he asks me what's for dinner. Jeez, it is like I have a child instead of a man. It's like I'm his waitress."

* * * * *

Autumn used to be a time for human migration, cooperation, travel, and togetherness. A time when Native American Indians would don their beaded and feathered deerskin clothing, their rabbit fur lined moccasins, take down their teepees or wigwams, and travel south toward winter's promise of a new home.

Autumn used to be a time of harvest – when every man, woman, and child would reap diligently all that they had sown - aside from the gleanings and the corners of their fields.

The intention of autumn is to be another turn of the proverbial page.

* * * * *

Susan was looking at me then as if I should have had all the answers. Unfortunately for her though, the answers I had were not the ones she wanted to hear. Although, as time would tell; she knew she needed to hear them.

* * * * *

September used to be a time when people would prepare for winter's long challenge of survival. When humans would smoke, dry, pickle, can, and jar away their winter stores. These days, autumn just seems to make people depressed for some reason. Perhaps when you remove the challenges from life, people tend to sour, spoil, and grow stagnant, malignant, and weak.

The change of seasons appears to fill some others with regret, but that is their fault, not the fault of the season.

* * * * *

"I once had a friend that married a man just because her parents did not like him." Susan shared with me.

I smiled. She paused.

"That's not what I did. I didn't do that."

And that's when I knew.

* * * * *

Autumn teaches us never to mistake kindness for stupidity, nor eloquence of speech for intelligence, nor humility with weakness, or faith with naiveté.

Autumn is reviving and revealing all at once.

Such a positively rich and aromatic season also teaches us to avoid mistaking immature behavior for basic human nature. With regard to human nature, it is true that we are always subject to temptation, subject to being tempted into making the wrong decision, especially when it comes to sex. Immaturity, anger, revenge, and sometimes desperation are the only things that will allow a person to make the wrong decision. Well, those and alcohol, and inexperience.

When you grow up, you do your best to stop making the wrong decisions, and that is the difference between growing up and growing old. Yet, sometimes when we do grow up, we still make the wrong decisions. It is all a matter of degree, and we are never finished growing up no matter what any older person says.

Either way, we need to stop confusing the two, and that is another thing autumn is happy to teach us. She teaches us the difference between death and pleasantly awaited change, and she teaches us the difference between growing up and growing old.

*   *   *   *   *

Autumn is a time for sweet remembrance, especially for those that overcome the hurdles of regret. Autumn is funny. Autumn is humorous. Autumn can even be hilarious at times. Anyone that has ever watched a child frolic in the autumn leaves knows exactly what I mean.

Autumn is the months in which a hug can heal a heart, the months in which a hug can often feel best. A time when soup is an elixir, hot chocolate, tea, or even a hot toddy can serve well a tortured soul, and a warm and open oven can make us feel like we are home.

Autumn is the sweetest meat, closest to the bone.

*   *   *   *   *

Susan had put on the full armor of the Lord, and she had turned to the word because she needed protection. What I did not know yet was that she still had not gone through conviction.

*   *   *   *   *

Autumn has a way, with her cheerful chrysanthemums and her never-to-be-rushed wild asters. She is saying, "Wait, wait… it is not over yet. Life is not done yet. Relax."

*   *   *   *   *

Human beings have a way of always turning off the music before the song is through. We push our plates away before the meal is over, rushing towards dessert. We seek orgasm instead of the loving embrace…

We all die a little older as far as our experiences go, though some of us may die very young.

September tells us there is such a thing as a very good apple.

If September had a sound, it might just sound like a softly baaing sheep, or perhaps the trill of a lone black cricket, the

25

rustling of leaves. September's fragrance is the smell of an entire mountain's essence carried downstream to the shoreline, into the streambed, grain by grain, and bit by bit.

Summer smells of sun tan lotion whereas autumn is the smell of sweetly wetted leaves.

* * * * *

At twenty-nine years of age, I thought I had finally become an adult. I was mostly alone but happily employed. I was going through many healthy changes.

I was still vulnerable to sin and self-deception, but I had begun to put away most childish things. I was sad at times, and I was lonely, but I was also joyful and content within the peace I had found with God. For the first time in my life, I could see why our ancestors had the foresight to include the pursuit of happiness among their fondest of hopes and dreams in our Constitution.

I was aptly poetic regarding my insight for a slowly aging, younger man, quite capable of appreciating a good football game and a cold beer, as well as a baby's first smile. I could pay my own bills with honor. I could take a young woman home without the offer of an illicit surprise. I was no longer prone to anger, nor was I frightful.

I could teach.

* * * * *

Susan put her cigarette out and said, "This morning I needed a ride to work. As you know, it was rainy and miserable. My husband was off from work today. Well, actually, he is unemployed, and he wanted to sleep in. He told me it would be 'inconvenient' for him to get out of bed to give me a ride in our car. We only have one vehicle and the night before he said he needed it."

She puffed away at her second smoke.

"Anyway, I had to walk to work in the rain. I cried the whole way and when I finally got to work no one could tell I'd been crying, thank God, because my face was all covered with rain."

What is her name? I must ask her…

While listening to her tale, all I could think about was the peculiar point that her husband had actually used a big word to offend her. *'Inconvenient.'*

God works in such mysterious ways.

Otherwise, all I could think was that I wanted to meet this man so that I might get the chance to put my boot in his ass.

* * * * *

Autumn offers the perfect opportunity to count our many blessings:

Me

You

We

Us

All of them

Everyone else

I never thought I would have the chance to see so many beautiful people, so many beautiful colors, so many beautiful faces, so many wondrous eyes…

* * * * *

I want to get to this point of maturity before I ever marry: I want to get to a point where I can look at one person and honestly say, "You are the one I love, and because I love you, you are the last person I ever want to hurt or offend. I am willing to do everything within my power to make sure that every one of your days are the best possible days they can be."

I want to be able to dedicate myself to the necessities of one human being, and *equally receive the same* from another. It should be one person, a single person for whom we do our best. That should be the goal. One soul to strengthen and support as opposed to torture and to take our pain out on, one soul to nurture, one soul to love and to understand as opposed

27

to hurt.

Many people do not believe such a marriage is possible, yet I have seen many, and each one is based upon a spirit of mutual respect and forgiveness, with two hearts focused on God.

* * * * *

Autumn is a time shared most closely between the dead and the living. If there are any grateful among the dead, who might they be, and for what might they be grateful?

I, for one, would like to count myself among the most grateful of the dead. It is my personal belief that the most grateful would be those who make it to heaven. For that, I would be most grateful, indeed.

* * * * *

"I'm sorry." I said these words so shyly I recall, "But we have been speaking this whole time and we still haven't properly introduced ourselves."

She covered her mouth and laughed. We both laughed, feeling somewhat childish and silly you could say, embarrassed; as if forced to acknowledge our childlike preoccupation with one another right there. It was all innocent, and we had not sinned, and yet; we were in more than one of many ways completely swept away by one another.

"I am Susan, Susan Watts. It's nice to meet you." She laughed again.

"My name is John," I smiled with her smallish hand in mine, "and it is nice to meet you as well."

* * * * *

Autumn is a time for the unbridled appreciation of God's most Holy creation: *everything around you and within.*

* * * * *

"Didn't you see any red flags, any signs that things might turn out this way?"

"Hindsight is always 20/20."

"Maybe you should invest in a new pair of glasses... or maybe even open your eyes."

We both knew I was referring to something higher.

Susan said, "I knew there was a reason I had to meet you today."

*   *   *   *   *

When I first noticed Susan in the lobby of our church, my eyes were drawn to her immediately. Nevertheless, as in many such cases, the Holy Spirit guided me away from introduction, reassuring me that our chance to speak would surely come one day.

We had made eye contact on many a fleeting occasion; and it was always the case that I was alone while she was deeply engrossed in some conversation with one of the older members of our congregation. I had never seen her with a man and each time I saw her I felt more and more compelled, even entranced by her. Yet, despite my predilections, I avoided contact as the Holy Spirit instructed me.

It was that "gut" feeling, and now I know why.

*   *   *   *   *

Autumn is a time of atonement and repentance, continued... Autumn is a time for giving thanks.

*   *   *   *   *

When I was in my early twenties, I was a bear. I don't mean that I was big and burley; what I mean to say is that I behaved like a bear.

Quite like the lumbering giant that is the bear, by force of nature and immaturity, I was willing to tolerate, even suffer, the multiple bee stings that accompany the indulgence of

29

sweet, wild sin. A bear may endure hundreds of bee stings in order to luxuriate in the consumption of wild honey, and so too would I whenever the opportunity would present itself. For me, it was always to indulge in a woman's sweet flower.

There were times, even weeks before I began to experience conviction, that I would welcome the lost into my arms, whether they were single and available, or not. I would fornicate madly, drunkenly, slovenly and unloving, even devouringly, all the while suffering those many stings.

I can remember not wanting to sit at a bar with my back to the door. Wondering whether some private investigator had photos, wondering and waiting for that dreaded moment when I would hear and feel the shot to my back as some forlorn husband whose trust I had so vainly abused pulled the small, black trigger of a gun.

I vowed such a thing would never occur again in my life, and again I made a vow that such a thing would never occur between Susan Watts and me. I would never do this, because for a man like me, that would be like a drug addict returning to the den. I could not have that, no, not at all, not after all I had promised to God, and certainly not after all I had been forgiven.

* * * * *

Autumn is a time for excellent slumber. Autumn is the time of sweet rest and better naps.

Autumn is a great time to awaken: refreshed.

* * * * *

Susan could not have weighed any more than a hundred and five pounds soaking wet when I first met her, although I never once made an attempt to pick her up.

Lift her up, yes, but pick her up, no.

* * * * *

Autumn reveals the special nudity of the woodlands, as her leaves stripped, procure a forest bare. Her grey granite boulders appear at once starkly, smoothly, as the half-dressed skeletons of tall, almost naked trees stand shameless in the detritus-strewn landscape of the spurious, natural world.

* * * * *

Susan swore up and down that she loved her husband even as she stubbed her third cigarette out on the ground and then moved closer. Her colorful blouse was dotted with rain.

One more step and I could feel my heart involuntarily begin to beat faster, and for a moment, I imagined it was time to go in.

"I'd like to have more of you inside me…" she said softly.

I wanted to cry out for help.

My facial expression tightening into one of concern, she noticed my reaction then, and smiled.

"Not like that. Not physically…"

My heart slowed as I let go my breath. Quite precariously, I was balanced on the edge of temptation and blaming myself for enjoying the feeling of positively thinking the worst.

Susan laughed and said, "What I meant to say was, well, I have never spoken with a man that could keep his eyes on mine without peeking, you know, without drifting, or with any man for that matter that would risk offending me by being as honest as you have been today. You are very direct John, and you speak the truth. That's how I know I can trust you, because you are not afraid to scare me away, yet, at the same time you don't scare me."

If there was ever a moment in time when I felt as if I had completely found the right woman for me, that was the moment. Yet, I knew in my heart that I could not have her. I think it was at that moment that Susan introduced me to the concept of loving a woman as a friend: for real.

I hated it, but that is what she had done.

* * * * *

Autumn is a time for introspection... and for letting things go.

* * * * *

"What I meant to say was, well, I think God has led me to you because honestly, so far no one has ever said to me the things you have said, and I think I, maybe I desperately need to hear what only you have been willing to say to me." She was glowing, "Other people might think it, but you are the only one willing to actually say it. What I need is your honesty inside of me. I think that is why I need you in my life."

I took a moment to warn her about the impropriety of an emotional affair. How such seemingly innocent affairs of the heart can be especially damaging during a time of strife within a marriage, and most specifically because she and I both attended the same church. Yet, I wanted nothing more at that moment than to figure out how we could know one another without causing any harm. Can that thin line become a reality? It's a dangerous path.

How can a single, Christian man, a man trying his best to be Christian, and a married Christian woman be... what is the word for that?

Is it "Friends"?

* * * * *

Autumn is a time for solidifying conclusions.

* * * * *

How does an ex-adulterous fornicator, a convicted lothario, convert to Christian living while retaining enough flexibility to survive?

* * * * *

Autumn is the time of year to observe the contrast of

32

skeletal, arboreal blackness set against the backdrop of a slowly setting orange sun.

Autumn is a time of great twilight awakenings.

* * * * *

"Would you be willing to talk to your husband about this conversation we are having?" I had to ask that.

That is the litmus test; the simple test that all wise people know how to apply. It is the formula of knowledge and wisdom. It is the elucidator of sin, and I knew right then that if she would not feel comfortable sharing the fact that we had spoken, and all we had spoken about, with her husband; that it was possibly the beginning of an emotional affair.

"Yes."

"Yes, what?"

"Yes I would feel comfortable telling my husband all of this. I have no problem with that."

"Good. Good." I felt somewhat relieved.

"There's only one problem."

"What's that?"

"I told you before: My husband refuses to have conversations with me. If I start to talk about anything, he just walks out of the house."

Damn.

* * * * *

Autumn is the time of year when fishermen reluctantly, yet eagerly, prepare for the kill upon the deep waters as the onslaught of colder weather makes their livelihood that much more a daunting chore. Meanwhile, hunters take to the snowy woods of latest autumn happily, contentedly, almost greedily eating up more.

Autumn is a time of abject differences.

* * * * *

"I don't know what it is." She admitted this despairingly, "He says he loves me, but he will not talk to me. He says he cares, but he doesn't give me anything I need."

"Have you ever told him these things?"

"He says he wants to be with me forever, but, at this point, what he is offering to me looks more like hell than a future."

Like a breast filled with dust in the hands of a crying infant...

"You should say everything you are saying to me to your husband."

"I've tried, but he won't listen to me. He keeps telling me I am *crazy*."

* * * * *

Autumn is the time in our almost circular, yet nonetheless elliptical orbit around the Sun when our particular hemisphere begins to tilt away from the source of all our light. It is a time of longing, the beginning of the cold.

Placed within are the deeper holidays, so we can experience a sense of much needed belonging, and so we do not fall apart.

The hell that often arises during the holidays can be cathartic, winter cleaning; a rebirth we most often fear. It is symbolic of all of our unexpressed fears of growing older while building up our debts of past regret.

* * * * *

Susan was only twenty-six. I was twenty-nine. I had been attending our church for one year, had experienced conviction three years prior – an experience that lasted an entire year – and then I found myself gratefully saved. Weeks later, I was born again in the sense that Jesus spoke of.

Susan had attended since her first wedding anniversary back in June. She did not attend regularly, but only when her schedule allowed.

Susan worked two jobs. I worked one. As soon as Susan's husband got a job though, he made her quit both to stay at home.

Susan said she received salvation two years prior, when she was twenty-four, although I had not yet asked if she had experienced conviction. I was not convinced she had.

* * * * *

Autumn is a time of great illusions: to our immature spirits, everything looks as if it has died, or is dying, or is just about to die.

* * * * *

She had such a beautiful voice... what man on Earth would not want to listen to everything a voice like that could say?

* * * * *

Autumn is a chorus sung by trees.

* * * * *

Was I headed for disaster just by speaking with this girl? Was I in trouble already?

I begged the Holy Spirit to act as my guide. I felt as if I was a child enjoying his first ride on a two-wheeler without training wheels, wobbly, unsteadily excited, looking forward with a mixture of want and fear.

The Holy Spirit stood beside me, and within.

* * * * *

Autumn makes the darkness of the lake look that much colder.

* * * * *

That night I thought about every other woman's face so I

would not dare envision Susan's. Even that did not work. Then Monday morning rolled around and I learned the church had hired me an assistant.

Can you guess who it was?

Yes. It was Susan's husband, Marvin Watts.

* * * * *

Autumn is tricky. Once August is over it gets cold. Then it gets hot, and then it grows warmer again. Then, just when you get used to wearing shorts and a sweatshirt, it is time to pack away your summer clothes.

Standing outside the gathering in the lightly falling rain, I turned to Susan and asked if she would prefer to go back inside. She had just finished thanking me for the fourth cigarette I had rolled for her.

"I don't mind the rain."

"Yeah, it's a blessing."

"A blessing, that's right! Just having it fall on you feels like a heavenly gift, doesn't it, as if God is pouring down His love upon you?"

We smiled in agreement. I prayed then that I would not discover anything more about this incredibly beautiful young woman that might further attract me to her.

We both felt the same way about rain.

* * * * *

Autumn is a time for self-discovery, and better yet, the rediscovery of others, and the rediscovery of our own hearts.

* * * * *

In our pause, while both of us admired the rainfall brightly, in that childlike manner, I tried to think of something I could say.

Nothing at first so rapidly came to me other then the words *I love you, Susan Watts.*

* * * * *

Autumn is the time of year best for dusting off the baking pans in preparation for the pie.

* * * * *

Back in early spring, they offered me the position of sexton of our church. The elderly man who had held the position before me had abruptly passed. He had held the job for many years. When he died, his assistant left and moved away.

My background in landscaping and building maintenance made me a perfect candidate for the job, and so they offered me the position and I gladly accepted.

It took me less than two months to get to know the old building all over, inside and out. I crawled through all the old passageways, through the attic and crawlspaces, and got to know and even re-labeled the aging fuse box. I discovered leaks no one had ever noticed before and I fixed them. I sealed cracks and tightened screws and made repairs that had slipped by the wayside some time before. I mowed the lawn and trimmed the many ancient hedges.

By spring, I had resurrected the church's long abandoned kitchen garden, and by August, we were dining on fresh melons, cucumbers, tomatoes, onions, squash and bittersweet herbs.

I planted sunflowers at the rear of the garden, zinnias and marigolds from seed, up in front.

* * * * *

Autumn is a time of reseeding, although we mortals usually think of that time as a time within spring. The Earth reseeds on God's own time, and it mostly does this in the fall when all the flowers die.

* * * * *

Susan asked if I would give her a tour of the garden and I gladly agreed. We looked at the fruit and all the many colors of the flowers while managing quite well to avoid any inappropriate flirtation.

Later on, once back inside the gathering, I chose from the desert table two portions of tiramisu – because the Holy Spirit told me to do so – and as told from on high that it would be this way; Susan joyously informed me that it was her favorite desert.

"How did you know? Out of all those delicious desserts, how did you know?"

"A little bird told me," was my answer. Then I thought of how that very bird had once descended upon Christ like a peaceful dove.

* * * * *

Little birds fly away in the winter, whereas all healthy robins depart in the fall.

* * * * *

It's different everywhere you go. For instance, if you live in the Southern United States, perhaps winter is a time when smaller birds arrive.

It's a different story everywhere and everywhen you go.

If we had lived somewhere else other than New England, and I do not know where such a place could have been, it may not have mattered so much that Susan had chosen to marry a black man. However, this was 1973, in a small town in New England, and the fact that I did not flinch or even blink when Susan first mentioned this to me, as I later suspected, had earned me a special place within her heart.

"I think it has a bit to do with why he will not attend church with me anymore. H-E-double-hockey sticks, people are looking down at me, not my husband, when we walk into a room. Why should he care? It's me they despise, not him."

I suddenly realized that either I was the first white male

from town she was expressing her thoughts to, or that perhaps she had systematically spoken with all the older men first, working her way down to the younger people in order to get a feeling for whether or not they would be accepted as a couple.

It was then that I realized I truly did have something valuable to say, so I said it. I said, "I dated a black woman once."

I was not lying. It had not been a lengthy relationship, nor had it ended very well, but I had firsthand experience with the pressures of the prejudice she was feeling. I thought it best that I should show her I could truly understand and relate to her predicament.

Her eyes lit up like candles when I revealed this, those two lovely, crystal blue eyes.

* * * * *

Autumn is a time for deeper knowing, and deeper sharing: deeper truths.

* * * * *

She spoke so rapidly I could hardly keep up with her.

"No one knows how hard he had it. He and his family escaped poverty. They escaped persecution, his great grandparents were slaves, and they are still trying to get out from under the weight of prejudice. No one knows what that is like. Do you know what I mean?"

I did not know, but I tried. It was then that I knew for sure that a white man who has dated a black woman does not know the first thing about what it must be like to be a white woman married to a black man. I hadn't a clue what that must have been like, to live like that in the eyes of a small, white town, and to feel that sort of pressure.

"No one else knows what it is like to grow up feeling like there is no love, no hope, not even a chance for happiness, and he overcame all that. He got out. And no one in this town knows what it is like to love someone like that."

That is when I had to stop her.

"Uh, Susan…" and I did not know how to say it, but I said it anyway, "I didn't date Michelle because I felt sorry for her, I dated her because I really liked her."

We had a momentary pause in our conversation just then.

* * * * *

September is the month of sins yet-to-be-revealed.

* * * * *

Susan stammered, and then politely asked me if I would roll her another cigarette.

* * * * *

Apple pies come with October, as do minced meats and pumpkins, spooky evenings and dripping dawns. September is a month more so dedicated to the first of the apples, the last of the watermelon, the ripest red tomatoes, and the deepening of the butternut squash.

September is the month in which the compost heap needs turning. Upon turning, the sinful sights and smells of our fetid past decisions and contributions to the world are eventually revealed. Yet, autumn also is a time for second chances. A time for reconciliation before the frost appears. A time of reckoning, a time of fruitful deliverance, and a chance for second chances at the glimmerings of truth.

* * * * *

I finally had to ask her, so I did. I asked, "Susan, have you experienced conviction?"

She swallowed hard as her eyes grew wider than a woman pretending to be a virgin on her wedding night, "I don't know."

My first thought was that there was not a soul alive that had ever experienced conviction by the Holy Spirit who could not answer the question with anything but the affirmative. Once experienced, and survived, the question is no different from being asked whether or not you own a car, or if you know your own last name. No one ever answers such questions with ambiguity or hesitation. I immediately empathized and felt for her.

"I don't think so," and she puffed on her cigarette, "Not yet. Maybe."

But she had not.

I tried to think back to the day my conviction began, to the moment, the very instant it began. The memory of the horror of it all, that most magnificently beautiful and terrifying moment of release… that day when I finally let go of the feted root of sin with my dirty palms in order to float downstream. That Day of Judgment, and conviction – to the verdict I was forced to say aloud – and it chilled me to the bone out there in the drizzling, blessed rain.

I thought of what my friend Bill, a Christian, had said to me when he saw what I was going through.

"Bill, you've got to help me. I think I am having a heart attack."

"What's wrong? Do you need an ambulance?"

"No. Bill, if this is the end, then I think I'd rather just die, but there is something I have to do first." I felt like a ghoul as I stood before him. *"I have to say I'm sorry to…"*

Bill had smiled knowingly as I sat myself down, relieved to hear me admit that I was willing to let God take me, to trust in God completely, if that was God's will.

I was so lost in sin I could not see. My backpack was full of boulders and stones. The mountain path was steepening, my wagon nearly overturning. I felt like a vampire and a zombie combined. I was a member of the walking, living dead.

"Bill, everything just started catching up with me – my sister the nurse, I called her a moment ago and she said it was probably just anxiety, but I think it is my sin Bill – I just realized it is all catching up with me now and the weight of it all is crushing me."

It was then that I recollected the words of a woman I had known years before, a woman who knew how devilishly bad I had always been, and the words she had chosen when she said, *"I'd hate to be around you when it all catches up to you. You know you are going to Hell, right?"*

That woman was no angel herself, a vile hypocrite in fact, but perhaps she had unknowingly planted a seed… the seed of Lazarus.

Bill laughed and said, *"You'd better take it slowly, my friend. No human being can face all his sins at once. It would surely kill him."*

My eyes must have widened, *"What is this, Bill? It feels like Hell."* I was looking down at my hands as if they were burning. I was far from speaking metaphorically.

Bill coughed and said, *"It is called 'Conviction by the Holy Spirit'."* Then he asked if he could pray over me. I gladly conceded, as I believed in my heart I needed all the help I could get. I was beyond a state of terror and the thought crossed my mind more than once that I might surely die before it was all over.

Bill looked at me and said, *"Brother, you've probably been fighting off this moment for years by using alcohol, pills, drugs, sex, rationalization, lies, and intellectualism… anything to pretend that there was never anything wrong with what you have been doing. And I know you have, because I know you."*

Bill was looking directly into my eyes and his eyes looked clear and bright to me. He was right. In fact, he was dead on.

"I know exactly how you have been living, John. You seriously need to get down on your knees and ask God for His forgiveness. If you do, He will be with you, and He will surely heal you. You will be saved. He will remove this burden from you, but if you don't, well then you might not make it through this thing alive."

The look on his face told me he was not exaggerating.

Then he laid his hands on my shoulders and said, *"In the name of Jesus Christ of Nazareth, who shed his blood for the remission of our sins: Satan, I rebuke thee. Lord, give this man the strength, along with a band of heavenly angels, to complete this course of conviction by the Holy Spirit, to repent for his sins, to be saved, and to carry on. Lord, I love this brother, and I ask you today in the name of Jesus Christ our savior who died on the cross for our salvation, to fortify this man for his repentance to come, and to keep him from the temptation of doing evil ever again."*

I felt better and I thanked him. As soon as he left, I looked up the word "repentance" in the dictionary. I then got down on my knees to pray and did not stop praying for nearly four hours; admitting everything I had ever done wrong, to God.

I shook off the memory, looking into Susan's eyes, and then I felt as if I had shed a joyful tear for her blessed conviction to come.

"You have been called..." I thought repeatedly.

*   *   *   *   *

Autumn is the perfect time to remember where you came from:

I came from God in Heaven.

I came from a sperm and an egg and there was definitely an orgasm involved.

I came from my mother's womb.

I came from a lower middle class family in the suburbs of a small city in the Northeast.

I came out of alcoholism and domestic violence.

I came out of laughter, good times, and fun, dirty jokes and cigarettes.

I came out of traditions, some healthy, some not.

I came from a sense of familiar, veteran patriotism and national pride.

I was born in a New England hospital and raised with an accent in a New England home on Anglo-Saxon American meals.

I was alive when McDonald's opened their first restaurant in my home town.

I saw the very first color TV's.

I am a child of God and His universe.

I come from the living, to dwell among them within this good life.

I am eternal, my soul immortal, but for now, I am alive.

* * * * *

Susan saw the teardrop forming in my eye and she shivered.

"What is conviction like?" she asked quietly.

The whisper of a rain that had been falling seemed to stop just then. A brilliant, natural pause to set the stage for what I was about to say. One blessing had ceased to fall upon us, perhaps as not to distract from the blessing that was soon to be revealed.

* * * * *

Autumn is also a time of many *last* chances: One more swim at the beach, one last day out there sunbathing, and one last ring of the ice cream man's bell.

* * * * *

I took a very deep breath and then I said, "It is like being submerged for an eternity in a bathtub full of putrid, fecal-strewn malarial waters and finally getting the chance to pull the plug and shower off. It is like pulling up a net and finding one large fish among many smaller ones, and deciding to throw the smaller ones back. It is like cleaning off your glasses and then looking at the world anew. It is like washing your dirty hands in warm soapy water. It is like spending a lifetime lost, and then finally finding your way back home."

Susan was impressed with my manner of speaking. She looked relaxed and interested in hearing more, "*Really?* What happens? What does it feel like?"

"Well, it feels like getting a 'do-over'. It feels like being born again, you are refreshed, restored, renewed even... and then after a very joy-filled interlude you realize that without wisdom, and without proper guidance, you could go ahead and

44

make the same mistakes again."

*　*　*　*　*

Autumn is the perfect time to redefine your definitions.

*　*　*　*　*

"It was my very first glimpse into forgiveness."

Susan looked a little confused, "What is the difference then," she asked, "between being saved or getting saved, and conviction and being born again?"

Hers was a very good question.

Without hesitation, I said, "Getting saved is like making it to home plate during the ninth inning in a ball game. Conviction is like having all the fans in the stadium point at you while shouting out everything you have ever done wrong in your life. It's very revealing."

Susan was shaking her head, "Oh, I don't want that then."

All I could do was to laugh.

"Why are you laughing?" Susan asked me.

"Because what you said was funny."

"Why was it funny?"

"Because within you is a record of your life, and if you have sinned, even once, you cannot have one without the other, and in the end, it is a beautiful thing."

"Then what about being born again?"

"That comes afterwards."

*　*　*　*　*

Autumn is a very good time to display how much you have truly grown… inside.

*　*　*　*　*

Biblical quotes were flowing through my mind at speeds beyond comprehension. I could see that Susan was thinking also. Then the faint, light rain returned to us, our precious blessing, our misty baptism, and it began to get a little chilly outside.

* * * * *

Autumn is a time for new beginnings. Autumn is a chance to say goodbye. Autumn is a chance for everything that lives to end one phase of life in order to begin another. Autumn is the perfect time to cry.

Autumn marks the return of shooting stars in great abundance.

* * * * *

Susan was shivering, but only a little.

Personally, I know in my heart that she honestly and sincerely believed our Lord is Savior, and that she loved His word, and very much desired it always. However, as it is with many people, the Lord, and the security she had found in His teachings, was not only sustaining her but preparing her to handle the inevitable, as well. Susan would experience conviction, but not just yet. Maybe not until she was just about to die, as with so many.

I for one prefer to have had this experience while I am alive.

* * * * *

Autumn is a leaf afraid of turning colors in the fall.

* * * * *

Susan would often stop and stare out into the distance as if looking for something to anchor her in the present, or perhaps she was just simply admiring the world around her. Sometimes I would watch her as she did this. Sometimes I would think that she was looking at the world as if none of it was real. As if her life was not real…

I asked her if she would prefer to go back inside, but she just started smiling after snapping out of her daze, standing there rubbing warmth into her arms, looking at me like I was nuts for even suggesting such a thing. I really liked her that way, just natural and beautiful, standing outside without a care in the world. Then she looked back at the church and asked, "Do you think anyone thinks we are out here getting friendly?"

I said, "It's a small town. You never know."

I can recall the year I moved to Shermansdale. I moved there shortly after returning home from college. I didn't want to move back in with my parents, and yet I didn't know where I wanted to go. So, I moved around for a couple of years, relying on my family's farm as a place to crash in between moves. Susan was reminding me that we were both interlopers in what most would consider a small town.

"I'm so used to people talking behind my back that I barely care at all anymore, I guess. I was just worried that people might start talking about you too."

"Me?" I said this as if she had awakened me from a dream. I could not care less for what other people thought. I didn't care, because I was with Susan.

* * * * *

Autumn is a time for the clarification of misunderstandings.

* * * * *

It was a fact that some of the people at the gathering had their eyes on Susan and me. They, those being somewhat unaware, did not fully understand that their eyes are truly the windows to their souls, and that from even across a crowded room their eyes can reveal their true intentions, and their judgments, and their thoughts.

Despite what many of them were whispering about us talking, Susan and I continued to talk publicly at the event, escaping every so often to indulge in a fresh cigarette.

I have always felt that it is fine not to care much for what

47

other people think. It is when you do not care what other people feel that you are treading on God's territory.

* * * * *

Autumn is a hot apple pie cooling slowly upon a windowsill. The needing and the mixing done in spring, the baking takes place during summertime. All that remains in autumn is the sweetness, the aroma, the savor. In winter, it is time to dive in and enjoy.

* * * * *

Susan had a terrific sense of humor. She not only got jokes, but could also make jokes as well and she did so as often as possible. The girl loved to laugh. The more I got to know her though, the more I noticed that some of her laughter was of the strained, forced, or even pained variety. The type of laughter that begs of one so in need of laughter they would pay any price just to eke out a smile, giving blood just to chuckle with a friend for any reason, anytime.

Those brief outbursts were some of the saddest moments I ever shared with Susan, although no one else in the room would have ever suspected a thing. The thing was; you had to know her to know the difference.

* * * * *

September is a very easy month to spell. It is not as easy as April, May, or June, but easy because you do not have to picture it in order to spell it. You simply let the word just roll right off your tongue.

Autumn is not like that.

* * * * *

The first time I ever noticed the difference between Susan's two kinds of laughter was at the end of the sentence she spoke concerning the fact that her husband did not permit her to watch TV or to listen to music without his consent. She tried to make such an example of disclosure sound like humor to me by adding the sound of laughter at the end of her sentence.

This did not impress me. Well, at least not in the way she had intended.

* * * * *

The Lord tells some trees to drop their leaves in autumn, along with the promise that they will return to them in spring.

September is the perfect month in which to listen to God's words.

It's all about trust... and trusting.

* * * * *

Susan was not weak: she was lost. However, she was by no means a victim; in fact, she was the crime.

There is nothing more entertaining from a spiritual standpoint than watching as a sinner nears his or her conviction. It is like watching a flower beginning to open, or a piece of fruit ripening on a tree. It is like watching a snowball rolling down a hillside, or in many cases, a spiritual and moral avalanche about to occur. At times, it can be a funny as watching a dog try to run up a slide. It can be as frustrating as a cat that is stuck in a tree. It is situational comedy, it is pratfall, and it is suspense.

Watching Susan, as she sat on the proverbial fence of her development, was like watching as a child approaches a present with the intention of opening it. There is that look of consternation mixed with joy, wherein they are lost in wonder as to whether it actually contains their hopes and wishes. You know the child is capable of opening it, yet they fumble with the wrapping. You know they will erupt with great joy upon opening it, yet the fear that it might just contain a bunch of socks keeps them semi paralyzed and confused, hesitant. It keeps them from getting their hopes up. They shake the box, then pause as the anticipation builds and everyone wants to shout, "Just open it already!" but the moment is too precious to destroy. As the child, perhaps even standing there in his or her pajamas sleepily, struggles with the will to enjoy rather than to just get it over with learns about want and then patience for the very first time.

That was Susan.

She had managed to turn her salvation into some sort of spiritual foreplay, and no one on this Earth was ever going to take that away from her.

What I did not know was that Susan needed a voyeur to make it all happen for her. She needed someone to watch her go through it. And as fate would have it, at twenty-nine, well, that is what I did best.

The Lord works in strange and mysterious ways, and all things done by God are done for the good of those involved.

* * * * *

September rhymes with remember.

* * * * *

It was August 28th and though I did not know it then, Susan was not planning to attend services on Sunday, the 31st. I would not see her again for another week. Perhaps that was for the best. In fact, it gave me some time to recover, and to pray…

"Sometimes I find it so hard to endure all the suffering in the world."

"Difficult."

"What?" and she laughed her true laugh.

"You find it difficult. Rocks are hard, concrete is hard, but experiences are difficult. They cannot be hard."

She laughed again.

I smiled, thinking I was so smart.

"Sometimes you take yourself a little too seriously, single man John. I was applying the second definition. Look it up sometime."

I did. She was right. She was also correct, resolute, and confirmed.

That was pretty much the last time I ever tried to correct her, and there we stood; level at the foot of the cross, more equal than before.

* * * * *

Spring is tough. Summer challenges. Winter is sleepy. Autumn is a time to be gentle. Well, all except for when chopping the wood.

* * * * *

"So, what do you find so difficult about all the suffering in the world?"

"Satan. That's the hard part. I mean, well, the Bible says it is going to be like this, at the end, you know."

"You think 1973 is the end times?"

"Sometimes."

"Go on."

"O.K., well, sometimes the way Satan runs this place just drives me nuts." She laughed, but I had a hard time discerning which one of her laughs this had been. I was not about to correct her, but I did want to offer my opinion on the subject.

"Satan?"

I had to think for another moment before I continued, "I don't think Satan is the cause of all the world's suffering." I said this without a smile, "People make choices and there are often horrible consequences and repercussions to their choices, but it is all people, not Satan. Satan can only tempt people to do wrong; he cannot make them do anything."

She cocked her head to the side in a way I will always remember.

I continued, "Think about it. Every single act of evil you could possibly name begins with a single human or a group of people making a choice. People choose evil of their own free

51

will, and God allows this, but to blame it all on Satan would just be silly. To blame it on God is even sillier. We need to retain accountability and affix blame where blame belongs. The blame needs to fall on the shoulders of the person who has made the choice."

Susan looked as if she may have been in shock.

"Then what about natural disasters?"

"Most of the time I think that's just nature, but then again, they do refer to them as acts of God. Satan doesn't have anything to do with any of that, and remember, when Jesus died He took the keys to Hell and now rules over Earth and Heaven at the right hand of God. Satan doesn't run anything except for Hell. Well, at least that is what the Bible says, anyway."

The truth is I still do not know why earthquakes happen except to say that it all has to do with plate tectonics. Even though people might die, I cannot see anything supernatural about them, nor could I then. Then again, you never know…

* * * * *

Why is it that alarm clocks sound so much meaner in winter and fall?

* * * * *

It was during that afternoon's gathering that I first learned of Susan's great love for poetry. She couldn't really name any poets, nor could she recite anything by heart, but from the way she talked about the subject one might have assumed she'd read everything ever penned in rhyme or verse.

"Footprints!"

She said she adored that one.

"Whitman?"

She hadn't a clue.

It was then that I made up my mind to buy her *Leaves of Grass.*

* * * * *

Autumn is the perfect time of year to take the path less taken.

* * * * *

The first thing I noticed about Susan was her face. Then, or maybe it was at the same time, her hair. Next, you could say it was her body. She was petite and I wondered if she was just thin, or whether she was suffering. (It would turn out to be the latter.) After that, I noticed her spectacular blue eyes. Shortly thereafter, I noticed her ring.

Then there was her voice, childlike and serene, sweet sounding, light, and playful. Then there was her thin, golden necklace with the little gold cross at the end. Her smile, again and again. Next, it was her laughter, and the subtle difference between her two laughs. Meanwhile, I was acknowledging the fear of impending conviction in her eyes; something she knew must have been coming and that really possessed me.

Her walk was intriguing. Her commitment to Jesus' teachings was irrefutable. Her ability to get along with almost anyone at all... well, this was remarkable to me.

The list only grew, and kept on growing.

* * * * *

September is an excellent month in which to take stock of the present. Actually, any day at all will fitly do.

* * * * *

Then there was her energy. Her cup was overflowing. She was the type of young woman that could plant a two-by-four with the expectation that a tree would surely sprout. She was contagiously hopeful, altogether inspiring.

Strangely enough, at least to me, she bore no distinction as far as fragrances go. There was no hint of perfume in her presence, a fact for which I am thankful to this day.

There was enough temptation already without adding scent to the mixture.

* * * * *

Autumn can make time appear everlasting. It is the perfect time of year to give some thought to eternity.

* * * * *

What else can I say? Having only known her for a short time, my observations were mostly physical; some were experiential, although in the minimal, with some remaining empirical. A few were speculative, even assumptive, and some were spiritual in nature, or by design.

Susan was nearly overpowering to my limited senses. Her mystique was immeasurable, her beauty, superb. However, I think what I enjoyed most was her long, curly hair.

* * * * *

Autumn is a very good time to admit just how small and insignificant we really are. When you are finished with that brief yet contemplative exploration, it is an excellent time to remind yourself how much God really loves you.

Susan's favorite dessert was tiramisu, and the next thing I discovered was that while I was in her presence, the Holy Spirit moved quite powerfully through me and through her as well.

We could complete each other's thoughts and finish one another's sentences from the very first start of our friendship. We could anticipate the other's direction. We always wanted a smoke or to change the subject at the very same time.

Strangely enough, we would apologize to one another often, even unnecessarily so, but not because apologies were often necessary between us, they were rarely called for, as we were both polite and considerate. Nevertheless, it had something to do with needing one another so desperately, for some unknown reason, that we were each terrified by the prospect of hurting the other, and so we pleaded for forgiveness at every turn, or so it seemed.

* * * * *

Autumn is the perfect time of year to count the seasons.

* * * * *

I started smoking in High School. Susan was sixteen. She smoked a lot. She spent a lot of time and effort trying not to cough in the presence of others.

* * * * *

Autumn is a child playing with an unlimited amount of crayons upon the canvas of the world.

* * * * *

I started drinking beer and whiskey in High school. Susan was sixteen.

I lost my virginity in High School. Susan was sixteen.

I lost my innocence in grade school. Susan was eleven years, three months, sixteen hours and thirty-seven minutes old to the moment, and try as she might, she would never be quite ready to forget that horrible day.

* * * * *

Autumn is a good time to let the past go while you still can, or to allow it to let go of you.

* * * * *

She said it had been raining very hard that afternoon...

* * * * *

Autumn gives us the opportunity to sit comfortably on outdoor furniture in long pants and a sweater with a woolen blanket over our legs while sipping coffee. If you ever get the chance, try the same thing with a hot Chai tea. You may find it wonderful, even life altering.

* * * * *

She told me she had gotten home from school about an hour and thirty-seven minutes before it happened, and that it was very dark outside, and raining.

* * * * *

Autumn somehow has a way of telling all the trees it is time for them to say goodnight, to say their prayers, to take one last drink of water, to drop their leaves like a colorful afghan to keep their roots warm and cozy over night. Some say the Sun does it, some say it is just God making one of his tougher decisions. Either way, it is not the end; it is only a change beginning.

* * * * *

She said she was home all alone that afternoon.

* * * * *

Autumn is the perfect time to count the shades of blue in the sky just before sunset.

* * * * *

I said, "I bet you must have hated God for letting that happen to you. Eleven years old... and right before your birthday."

* * * * *

Autumn is the perfect time of year to slow down and take that very deep breath you have been waiting for all of your life.

* * * * *

She began to tear up for the third time that day. The gathering was still growing inside, the blessed people accumulating in greater numbers.

* * * * *

"I bet you really hated God back then."
"I did," and the tears began to fall in great abundance with this admittance.

* * * * *

Autumn will not come around forever.

* * * * *

Susan said, "That day was really crazy. She was always home by four-thirty. That's how I knew that something was wrong."

* * * * *

September sings a lullaby, softly bespeaking of down... downy soft feathers blown on the wind or deep asleep within your pillow. The last of the fleeting dandelion puffs scatter beneath the clouds as soft as whispers, then hauntingly a thousand leaves may skitter as they hurry on their way across the road.

* * * * *

"And we did not own a phone, so I couldn't even call anyone. Even so, who was I to call back then?"

"You must have *hated* Him."

* * * * *

If winter is made of diamonds, and spring is made of emeralds, then summer is fashioned from fire, and autumn, from the dreams of little girls and boys... even the bad ones.

* * * * *

"I was home alone all night, even until the morning, because I was too afraid to leave the house for all the thunder and the rain."

"*Please don't tell me she... Please.*"

Her crystal blue eyes were exploding with watery light when she said this, "The sheriff's deputy found her car early the next morning," she said this as her hand made its way across her face and began to tremble.

* * * * *

Autumn is the perfect time to say, "Sweet dreams... I love you... goodnight."

* * * * *

"I hated you, God. I hated you so much for letting that happen!"

* * * * *

Autumn can make any distance feel that much farther away.

* * * * *

"Her purse must have flown out the window and it must

have flown pretty far away from her vehicle, because they didn't even know it was my mom until late that afternoon. I didn't know what to do. I just ate breakfast and walked to school even though she had not come home the night before."

* * * * *

Autumn can often be a time for early snowfall. A time when we are caught off-guard, ill prepared for all that is to come. Autumn is a time for sad surprises, sad surprises and for reassessing… and for reassuring love's existence in our lives.

* * * * *

"I walked to school with wet leaves stuck to the bottoms of my penny loafers. Then I just sat at my desk in my classroom and cried. I thought she had abandoned me. I could not even explain what was wrong to my teacher."

Susan paused to wipe away two dozen more tears.

"It wasn't until the sheriff showed up at my classroom door in his dark, shiny black raincoat that I knew something must have been wrong."

As I listened to Susan tell me her story, I could not speak a word. All I could think was, *"No… no, you can forget my past. Nope, I have never suffered… I have never really had my heart broken before. Not like this, Lord… not like Susan has."*

Then I began to count my many blessings, deep within my soul.

* * * * *

Autumn is the time of goldenrod and rainy Mondays.

* * * * *

We had stepped outside for another one of our sacred cigarettes. The Sun was finally settling down and Susan was sharing with me the story of how she lost her mother back when she was in the fifth grade. The fatal accident occurred at 4:37 pm on a Thursday, but she did not get the message until the following day.

The night before, the evening she had to spend all alone in solemn wonder, crying herself to sleep between prayers, waiting, was not nearly as rough and cold as the next one that November in the fall.

*   *   *   *   *

Autumn is the loneliest time of year for the color blue.

*   *   *   *   *

Within Susan's eyes I saw the desperate need of that lonesome and frightened fifth grader still trapped somewhere inside her tiny frame, and it took every ounce of my Christian strength not to want to rescue her. Instead, I simply continued to offer my ears.

*   *   *   *   *

Autumn is a snake's pale skin… shed for growth beneath the twigs among the stones.

*   *   *   *   *

For a single man with no family of his own, Susan became the bridge for me to learn about loving unconditionally, along with healthy boundaries of course, so that I might someday love a family of my own. Every man should have one, one woman, a female friend that can teach him that love need not be casual or sexual: none of the above. What Susan showed me was that love is all of the above, and in the end, should be nothing from below when it comes to true friendship. The rest you can share with your spouse, with him or her only.

* * * * *

Autumn is the darkness that befalls each and every one of us, shortly before the ever-present, softly falling white.

* * * * *

Susan used to dream of being a princess. That dream lasted for eleven years until that cold November morn.

* * * * *

Autumn is the guillotine of soft machines that puts the kibosh on summer's base desires.
Autumn is a slowly burning fire in the dark.

* * * * *

Susan tried to commit suicide by the tender age of twelve. Now that is the definition of pre-adolescent Hell.
Maestro, I ask you, what has gone wrong with this sweet song of spring, and of youth, in this holy cathedral?

* * * * *

September days are crazed because you do not know which way to go, nor where it is that you are going. Voices change, the blood runs red, the kids grow up and college calls, and where did all the time go?
September days are crazy when you do not know which way to go, or which way it is that you are going.

* * * * *

That is when Susan showed me why she prefers to wear turtlenecks. I could have cried for her then if it were not for the shock.

*   *   *   *   *

Autumn is an orange peel drying in the sun, whereas summer is a plump ripe purple plum.

Youth should be more like getting to lick the spoon before the cake goes in the oven, than discovering why it is a mother should not drink and drive.

*   *   *   *   *

There stood Susan Watts, like the little monkey face hidden deep within the slice of fresh banana – bananas, milk, and sugar – the makings of a princess' dream, or even a prince's. Youth should be like getting to lick the bowl while your mother does the rest of the work and looks on laughing, but for Susan, that one sweet dream had come undone.

*   *   *   *   *

A basketful of autumn, the remnants of the summer's sun, all encased within a coffin of dried flowers. From the foundation of a child's tiny shoes, how the trees must look so tall and overgrown...

*   *   *   *   *

Susan and I have never made love, although together we did generate plenty of it. It all began the moment Susan finished telling me about her mother's untimely demise. There was no father involved, so it had only been the two of them.

I do not enjoy feeling sorry for people.

*   *   *   *   *

Autumn is the awaited return of a ragged, long lost friend... even one you have not met yet.

*   *   *   *   *

It took a while for things to start changing, but that was the last time Susan ever firmly held anything against God. Susan was a survivor, she lived her life like a firefly on the chilly side of a mountain, face turned toward the windy currents, intermittently aglow.

* * * * *

The first day of September is like taking a break on the hiking path of existence in order to empty your backpack. The second day is like getting back up and heading on down that road.

* * * * *

"I love cleaning," she said to me, quite possibly to change the subject.

That is just one of the lesser tidbits I recall from our conversation that evening.

"I love getting rid of it all... just throwing it all out. Cleaning house, making room for all the newness, you know? I just love it when I can walk through our house when no one else is home and feel the crisp, clean, undisturbed carpet beneath my bare feet. I evaporate in it all." She smiled feigningly, even disdainfully, "I hold on to that, because in that moment I know our house is mine. That is when I know our house is really our home. I feel like it is ready for everything that is going to happen."

Her pause felt like a funeral.

"It is part of my peace and seclusion. It is part of all the best that saves my soul apart from Jesus."

I had never before witnessed a woman trying so hard to stay in love.

* * * * *

Autumn is a kick in your patched up old blue jeans. Taken correctly, it can get you up and dancing. You will dance until you are weary. Dance away every day until you are finally done.

*   *   *   *   *

"Be careful not to start the word in the middle of the page, unless He points your finger there to help you with your rage. Or your loss. Or your heartache. Or your sin…"

*   *   *   *   *

Within a year, my sweet Susan; the one woman I could love, but could never have, went from loving poetry, to becoming a poet… then, from becoming a poet, to becoming a poem as well.

She had my heart bound up in chains, secured with earthly shackles bound by starlight memories and verse, but as I had vowed, she would never know this, nor would I ever touch her.

*   *   *   *   *

Autumn is a time for sweet release. Rejoice without ceasing, may your rejoicing never cease.

*   *   *   *   *

"Do you have any idea what that means?"

"What?"

"That pause we just took?"

"What does it mean?" I was being coy, and I was smiling, because I already knew.

"It means I can trust you."

"Really? How so?"

"I know I can trust you because most men would have taken that as an opportunity to reach out and try to kiss me."

*   *   *   *   *

Autumn can creep up so amply, so carefully and so slowly, that it could make an old fisherman retire out of his envy of its patience.

* * * * *

She prayed, "Thank you Lord. Thank you for letting me work with my mother – to do this work for her – to sing with my pen in the memory of her name."

I had no idea that she wrote all her poems for her mother. They were poems of heartache and a great love; one liners about each of the four seasons... Secretly, I had always wished they were for me.

That blasphemous lothario still dwelled within my heart. There I sat, repenting again, "Sorry Lord, but I am trying."

* * * * *

Autumn is a time for second, second chances. Thank the Lord.

* * * * *

She said, "I do one-on-one battle, and not because the Lord demands it or commands it, but because I drag myself out onto the battlefields where such battles can be won."

I could have died right there that evening. She had been fighting so hard and for so long that I never once believed in all my life that I might see such strength displayed within a living woman. She was a warrior amidst racists and sexists, a social exorcist. She was a reformer of spiritual thieves, a woman who would not cease in her efforts until she could quicken the spirit and body with truth.

For one poor moment, Susan almost became my idol.

* * * * *

Autumn is a costume: nature's mortal coil shuffled off

discretely, slowly, enticingly, like a burlesque, twilight storm approaching from the east.

* * * * *

I found myself illicitly indulging in the fact that Susan had so deeply confided in me that I had to ask her husband's name, just to keep myself from running away and saying goodbye for her sake, for his sake, and for mine.

"It's Marvin. Marvin Watts."

* * * * *

Autumn is the pear that bears your name, whose buttery, brandied accoutrements once consumed and passed your pallet, leave you satisfied and never wanting to be the same, never wanting to be that same again.

* * * * *

Susan saw me changing right before her eyes. It was a change in my attitude and she quickly changed the theme of her story, and so I remained.

"The very next year I planted a garden."

Once again, I was lost in her eyes.

* * * * *

Autumn is the time of year for breaking out the can of oil. Dorothy knew, just ask the tin man.

* * * * *

"Have you ever heard of an English garden?"

"Would that be a garden in England, or a garden that speaks English?"

I actually got her to laugh that beautiful laugh, and for a moment, I was proud of myself. I felt glad.

"No, Silly. It is a garden in which you simply throw seeds and bulbs, and that is all. No planning, no form."

"Sounds wild… I kind of like that idea. It sounds kind of like the way God made the world."

* * * * *

In autumn, most everything with seeds drops their blessings and their promises to the ground as a gift to the future. They simply throw their gifts away and trust in God that there is a plan.

* * * * *

Susan went on and on and I let her. She flowed like water, so fluently, never stagnating, so altogether passionately it would have been a sin to ask her to stop talking about her many interests, even her complaints. She was lifting herself out of the memory of her mother's death with tales of poetry and gardening, and it was beautiful to watch her tend to her cares. She had progressed through twilight into the bitter darkness, then back into the light of day, and then there we were standing out there all alone, together in the mist as darkness approached.

* * * * *

Autumn is the season of the haunted crescent moon, as the rusty clock strains purposefully to complete its final hour.

A pin stuck through a teardrop; the crumpling of paper about to burn, tossed into the fire, the finality firmly held within a shooting star.

* * * * *

Angels flew down mercifully. Lightning crackled up above. I wrote a song for her in my heart that evening, but I could not release it, save for a love that knew that such a song might be misconstrued, less edited from above.

I was a lamb that night. A lamb unfit for sacrifice due to the multiple blemishes on my heart. I could have fallen in love that evening. Instead, I chose a stronger path, and as she and I stood out there beneath the Pleiades – beneath the sparkling late august sky – I committed myself, once again, to believe in her, and despite my earthly father's crimson words, I said goodbye without ever touching her.

* * * * *

Autumn is a time for long, slow dances, trepidations, romances, even risking it all when falling in love. Autumn is a time for sacrifice, not often kind, not often nice. In the end, the coin toss and the bloodshed allows us to understand that we had not nearly enough holiness as children, even in our parent's eyes.

God Save the Queen, and may God save our president, and anyone else for that matter that has the power to decide what might happen to our precious lives and futures.

God save the Queen by saving her soul... so she won't treat the peasants like trash.

* * * * *

Autumn is an iceberg, just about to break. Autumn is a fist unclenching, drunk before the wake. Autumn is a man unaccustomed to wearing a tie. Autumn is the sweet bosomed woman that blesses you before you die. Autumn will dare you to cry, even to try, if you will let her.

* * * * *

I was falling in love and I had to get away. Susan was too much for me. Beautiful, gentle, kind, and well spoken, generous, gracious, and unbelievably sound. Creative, energetic, spiritually willing, compelling; she possessed that caliber of class that told me she would one day instruct her daughters that they may often feel in such a way, but that it would be far less than lady-like and far beneath them to ever act in such a way. I was sure she could also raise boys.

* * * * *

Autumn is a time for target practice.

* * * * *

And that's when Susan turned to me and whispered, "Teach me something new. Could you? Teach me something I do not know, and make it something interesting, or make it anything at all."

* * * * *

Autumn is the quiet song in the voice of the willow.

* * * * *

I chose to teach Susan how to make a cricket's call, but she could not manage it at first.

"It's like this: you have to hum in a way with your lips and whistle at the very same moment."

"Chiree. Chirp, chirp, chirp, chiree," as I mimicked the sound of a cricket.

She giggled at the sight and sounds of me.

"It's easy once you get it: Chiree, chirp, chirp, chirp, chiree," as I smiled in the dark of nightfall, "Try again."

She tilted her head and stared at me as if amazed and then she laughed. Susan's eyes twinkled with the starlight as the natural world and all its crickets laughed at me as well.

* * * * *

Autumn bows down to placidity and serenity as if it had two knees.

* * * * *

After a few more tries, amidst our frivolous, almost flirtatious laughter, Susan finally got it. Then she was off and trilling as a cricket might beneath an August Moon.

* * * * *

Autumn is a rusted red shovel lying in the sand. Autumn will take you by the hand and lead you wandering.

* * * * *

I have never seen a woman become so childlike that the wild side of it all was slightly scary, while all along the tenderness and safety of it all remained so clear.

* * * * *

I rarely allow myself to look at the things,
the things we were in the yesterday.
It is here,
it is here I tell myself,
it is here that I must stay.
I do not allow myself to dream of things,
the things we used to dream.
All the many things we dreamt
that we would one day be.
It would play on me
to appeal to yesterday,
ever since you sailed away
into the light
that we wished that we could see…
Oh why,
oh why Mom,
did you have to go?
What was it you just had to know?
And maybe,

70

oh, it sounds so crazy
but maybe you could send me a sign
that all those things,
those funny things we believed in
might all turn out to,
will all turn out to,
turn out to be true.
How there might still be room for you and me.
And maybe,
that we weren't all so wrong,
saying all our prayers,
and singing all our songs…

* * * * *

Autumn isn't always easy.

* * * * *

Susan tucked the cricket verse I had taught her into her pocket, and then she taught me how to be a stronger man.

* * * * *

Autumn is a blue balloon on a Sunday afternoon.

* * * * *

Susan began to read the song in the words written in the stars and the pain written in my eyes:

I was not responsible for your death.
I never made that sacrifice.
I only tried to help you, to share with you my free advice.
When I met you, you were broken, half-broken from the start.
I never knew you truly, but I swear I knew your heart.

Susan read the song again and it was as if we were traveling through time together out there under the stars. There were no words to describe it all. No words left to us at all.

* * * * *

Autumn is a broken heart that sees no happy ending.
Winter is the purifying white.

* * * * *

At that point, neither one of us could tell why we had been brought together. All we knew was that God had done something mysterious and powerful of which we were a part. We both loved the rain. Together we adored the stars.

* * * * *

Autumn is a harvest time for so many forgotten fears.

* * * * *

All the rivers flow into the sea and yet the sea is not full… but how can one tell when autumn is full? When there is not a single leaf left on any tree.

* * * * *

Autumn is just one of the many prices we pay. Autumn may not have a lot to say, yet it speaks volumes about the value of spring.

* * * * *

Susan loved autumn as much as I did, and she wrote so many poems about it I could not count them. When we met, on that fateful August afternoon, she told me that her husband Marvin thought that autumn was little more than a chilling reminder that all of us would eventually die.

72

I was surprised. I said, "To me it always feels like the start of school."

"Me too! So many people consider the seasons to be dreadfully symbolic: spring is the child, summer is life, autumn is growing older, and winter is death. I don't like thinking about it that way. I think each season has a life of its own, sometimes. At least every season bears its own fruit."

Hung up on the death thing, I said, "I don't see death as a bad thing. In fact, death to me is the doorway to heaven."

"So you're more of an apple pie kind of fellow."

"A la mode."

* * * * *

Autumn is the perfect time to try Mexican vanilla ice cream. You'd be surprised to know that it is brown.

* * * * *

The year was 1973 and the Vietnam War was just barely over. I was wearing plaid slacks and Susan was dressed in bell-bottomed jeans and a psychedelic blouse. It was 8:45pm and we had switched from wine to Cokes. If she had not been married, I would have asked her out right then, but she was married and so I settled for a form of Christian admiration, coupled with good conversation, that I can only define as two being friends. It was the beginning of a friendship blessed from above by Heaven, at times cursed from Hell below.

* * * * *

Sunflowers take their bows the first week of September while the Queen Anne's lace curtseys her goodbyes. Meanwhile, the Monarchs head for Mexico, to dance upon the trade winds, to play in the misty rain. These simple dances remind us that, while we are yet innocents, surely we are drafted into sin with great pomp and invitation.

* * * * *

The following Monday morning, Susan's husband came to work for me as assistant sexton of the church. Winter was coming, everyone could tell it was going to be a bad one, and the board of our church thought it best that I have a hired hand to help me prepare for the cold.

No one ever asked me if I even wanted assistance from a helper.

Marvin Watts' experience with yard work was limited to his experiences in his own backyard, and that backyard had been a mess, an eyesore within town. Not much of a yard at all. Fortunately, he had worked in a hardware store in the city, so he knew his parts and he knew his tools and materials well. He was strong and he seemed willing. He had also been in the army and gone to war. He was also, as I would soon discover, intelligent and resourceful. Despite the fact that it often wounded me to acknowledge that I had never met a woman I could relate to as much as his wife, and that he would not give her what she needed, let alone even talk with her, I actually took a liking to him rather quickly.

Shortly before Christmas though, he lost his job.

How? Well, it is not what you might think. It mostly had to do with politics within the church, and Marvin's predilection towards sinning. Nothing illegal ever really occurred, although immorality most certainly applied.

* * * * *

Autumn makes it harder to hide in the woods, yet for others, it provides for a very sporting hunt.

* * * * *

Susan's husband was cheating on her.

Possessing this knowledge was crushing to me.

To some men, such information might prove to be handy, might even serve as the key to open the door to an illicit affair.

74

Nevertheless, I would not sin with her, and I would not risk destroying what was left of their marriage for a thin slice of fun. I could not do it, not after all the Lord had done for me. The thought did cross my mind though. The problem was I simply loved both the Lord and Susan way too much for any of that.

* * * * *

Autumn is a time for the closing of heavy doors.

* * * * *

Marvin began working with me on a Monday. I discovered his secret the following Friday, and saw Susan for the second and then the third time that very same Friday and the following Saturday afternoon.

Susan was so much lovelier than her husband's lover ever could be.

* * * * *

Autumn is our first great glimpse into the perpetuity of renewal. It is our first peek into eternity and our very first lesson in hope.

* * * * *

Marvin Louis Watts and Teesha Jane Daniels were both semi-tallish Ethiops, equally beautiful in that dark skinned, polished way, and I will admit that on more than one occasion I had secretly wished they would run off together forever, but they would not.

Consumed by the fire of their affair, impassioned by the very nature of its incorrectness, they were like two bird watchers that would never raise a bow.

* * * * *

Autumn is a time of heavy sweaters.

$$* \quad * \quad * \quad * \quad *$$

Marvin called off early that Friday, just prior to the afternoon.

Be careful whom you hurt and how you hurt them…

He told me he had some family business to attend. He should have referred to it more appropriately as a "family affair."

They met down by the bridge that crosses Mulley Creek. The leaves on the trees had not yet begun changing.

$$* \quad * \quad * \quad * \quad *$$

Autumn is a time for listening closely to the soft crunch of tiny stones beneath your feet while slowly strolling down the road.

$$* \quad * \quad * \quad * \quad *$$

My interest in Susan blinded me to wonders, even deafened my ears to the voices of angels and the messages of God. The fury I felt over her husband's deception, the rage I felt over how he could deny her, even ignore her, kept me tormented inside nearly every single day. I found it nearly impossible not to think of her, or while I was working out there with him, not to somewhat lose my mind.

Meeting this pair was like getting both ears boxed in and both eggs kicked in at the very same time. However, it took weeks before I realized how immensely distracting their dilemma could be.

I stopped praying, unless of course it was to pray for her, or to pray for his redemption and salvation, or to pray they'd get divorced. I no longer read my Bible, unless it was to find a quote for her, or so that I might reread Jesus' thoughts concerning the coveting of another man's wife, and adultery.

By the end of September, I was nearly in complete and utter

76

spiritual ruin. She and the memory of our first meeting haunted me. We could not even sit together in church, even though she attended services alone.

Yes Lord, I had become just a little obsessed.

*   *   *   *   *

Autumn is a time for faith, coupled with the clearest of admissions.

*   *   *   *   *

The way she used to look at me; that long distance affirmation from across a crowded room was more than I could handle many Sundays. Hers was a look that said, "We will have to wait until we are in heaven to finally express this love."

*   *   *   *   *

Autumn is the time of year when nature brews her wine in fallen apples and grounded berries. A time of year when bears get tipsy, deer walk sideways, and many a drunken raccoon will delightfully stay up all night.

Autumn can be a time for poorer decisions.

*   *   *   *   *

Every Friday, Marvin left work shortly after noon. He would wash the rusty grease or soil from his hands and fingers, change his shirt, smile, tip his cap, and drive away.

She would meet him down by the bridge, and sometimes I would watch them, even watch as his beat up old car would bounce and rock around by that crossing.

There were times when I wanted to take a photograph, but I could never do that to her.

*   *   *   *   *

Autumn is a wonderful time to return to somewhere you have forgotten.

* * * * *

When the first leaves began to fall, I walked down to that old stone bridge that crosses Mulley Creek, separating the church's thirty-two acres from the dairy farm next door. I had a stick in my hand that I used to carry with me on my walks.

Marvin's tire tracks were still visible in the mud. Aside from me and them, no one else every really went back there.

I smoked two cigarettes and threw a few crabapples and a couple of rocks into the creek there. The sky was grey, somewhat fish-scaled, and lowering. I walked away with my head down after spotting what they had left on the side of the road there.

* * * * *

Autumn is a time for pulling up bootstraps and turning away from anger, among other nominal sins.

* * * * *

By October, I had to stop drinking entirely, but that didn't last very long.

I had been saved in '71, but had held onto the smokes and my occasional forage to the tavern. However, I did not put down the pint glasses for reasons of salvation. I put them down due to a dreadful fear of falling even deeper into what I often hoped could be described as love... while I was drinking. I began to fear that I was simply obsessed with having something, someone I could not, and that someone was Susan Watts.

That someone was another man's wife.

They say the first step to solving any problem is admitting that you have one. My problem was not booze; it was what I allowed myself to do or think once I started drinking. What I would do was to pine over Susan. That was wrong, and yes, it was a definite problem.

*   *   *   *   *

Autumn is to evening as winter is to night.

*   *   *   *   *

It all started happening for the worst just a few hours after that afternoon I spent throwing apples and rocks into Mulley Creek when the leaves first started falling. Driving my truck to the tavern afterwards, all I could see was Susan's face, Marvin's smile, that rockin' and rollin' Caprice Classic, and that disgusting reminder in the weeds by the side of the road. I went into the barroom, found a barstool, and there I sat to stew in my anger. I felt evil all over, dirty and wicked inside.

I was mad.

The barmaid was lovely, yet I could not even think of her, let alone admire her. Three pints later, I felt something inside of me dying. I could feel myself willfully separate from my spirit as I rejoined my sinful self in the darkest of regrets and even deeper lamentations. Songs floated through the air, but the tone and message of each did not help my mood then. I emptied an entire pack of rollies, purchased a pack of Camels, and even ordered myself a shot of Bourbon or two.

I was like a man on a mission to lose his sanity in public so that I might not be responsible for the things I might have done, or might just have chosen to go ahead and do, after a few.

I did not share the word or any jokes with any of the other patrons. I hardly even acknowledged that anyone else was there. Drinking, sitting, staring ahead at my view of the wall disrupted only occasionally by a close up of the barmaid, I drifted off into something I did not care to be. I prayed, but ignored all the answers. Then I did my best to convince myself that Susan would discover Marvin's infidelity on her own, leave him, and then after some time of healing, eventually come to me. How we would eventually marry, in time.

I sat there and dreamt miserably about how her second walk down the aisle would turn out to be the right one, the good one, and the correct one. If only she had been more patient the first time around. I dreamt of how we would finally be together, and have our lovely children. Then I almost got impatient myself, but most certainly went a little mad.

*　*　*　*　*

Autumn can be an awful reminder that fire, killing, and defending one's own can mean the difference between death and survival.

*　*　*　*　*

The Friday evening after I discovered Marvin's secret romance was difficult for me, but even more so difficult because Susan had shown up at the church around four-thirty that day, shortly after Marvin and his passenger had moved on.

Susan was wearing a homemade prairie dress with a thin white turtleneck beneath. Many other men in town would not even look at her since she had chosen to marry a 'Colored', a black man, yet this made absolutely no difference to me. I no longer saw color in Christ.

It was a difficult afternoon, and hard for me, because I had to avoid the subject of Marvin altogether which was one of Susan's favorite topics, and I had to steer her in the direction of the mundane amidst small talk in order to keep myself from screaming out the truth.

That Friday eventually turned into the night of the seventeen pints.

Later, I passed out in my truck after getting sick once out the door. By morning, I discovered I had even wet my pants. Seventeen pints and how many shots of Bourbon, I do not know. The next morning I felt horribly alone and ashamed.

I had completely respected Susan outwardly, but in my heart

and in my mind, I had certainly coveted her tremendously. I had sinned against God and His kingdom. I had not sinned because I was attracted to her, no. That is not a sin in God's eyes. I had sinned because I had plotted to bring ruination to her marriage, and not because I wanted to help her. My sinful heart's intention had been to make her mine.

I woke up colder than alone.

* * * * *

Autumn is a time for sealing secrets away in the ground. Winter resurrects our secrets and prepares them for the haunt.

* * * * *

I buried my heart in the gravel parking lot of that tavern, started my truck, and drove away cursing myself, the stench of vomit, and the wetness of my jeans.

* * * * *

September is only one of twelve opportunities for forgiveness.

* * * * *

Before I left for the tavern, Susan had asked me what was wrong.

* * * * *

Autumn should have been a time for honesty.

* * * * *

I attended church that Sunday noticing that Susan was not there. I kept turning my head to the left and to the right until the sermon was finally over. I cannot recall a thing the pastor had said.

The feeling enveloped me – that dull poison entered me – even worse than my hangover the day before. Sickened by the idea that I had not seen her, I left the church with my head down.

Earlier, I had walked in quietly and had sat down in a pew within two paces of my regular location, although at the time I did not even bother to look for her. I thought for sure she would be there, and that I would speak with her afterwards. Talk to her outside in the parking lot; even join her for a smoke in the yard with the other more visible sinners and folk.

I had no idea how much damage not seeing her could have done to me, until it happened that day.

* * * * *

October, often noted as a time for accepting candy from strangers, we prance around in demon masks. Temptation preys. Despite the levity of souls whose eyes have seen with hearts glimpsing Holy, the demon remains inside to lure us astray.

* * * * *

Once I told Marvin that I knew what he was doing. Marvin only laughed and said, "What? You jealous, man?" It was in that moment that I could have sworn he was Satan.

So why did I feel like I was more guilty than he was?

* * * * *

Autumn is a very good time to simply turn and walk away.

* * * * *

Halloween has never been a very big holiday for true Christians in many parts of this country. In fact, it is considered a pagan holiday at best and by most. What many

82

Christians do is to celebrate the harvest.

Susan was on the committee that would bring to fruition a party on the 31st, nearly two months to the evening on which we had first met. It was up to me, the trusty sexton, to help them with the details, and this would mean that Susan and I would be working very closely together for a span of two days.

Little did I know that Susan was nearly as tormented as I was, equally if not more steadily falling for me as well. Somehow, her heart knew what her husband was doing, and she had become deeply frightened by that.

* * * * *

October can be a time for keeping distances.

* * * * *

The difference was that I had coupled my love for Susan to lust, whereas her growing love for me more closely resembled an emotional need.

* * * * *

The powder blue chicory flower makes its last appearance in September just as the sumac blossoms complete their lofty blush. October then christens autumn with frosty dew upon the morning; pumpkins shiver as the apples reach perfected firmness, unmatched in nature, as all the maple leaves appear glazed by sugar crystals of pure white on the ground beneath the sun.

* * * * *

During the second day of decorations, Susan broke down. Once we had found ourselves alone in the sanctuary, she cried, but she would not admit what was wrong. She would only proclaim in a very soft voice that she was due for, and in need of, a hug. A very big hug.

I declined and distanced myself from her, compassionately, or so I thought. She did not appreciate my response.

As she stated her case, I stood explaining how inappropriate it would be for us to embrace even in a Christian fashion. How awkward and imposing it might turn out to be if even the smallest and most innocent of eyes were to happen upon us, and to see us. Yet, all I really wanted was to hold her.

That afternoon, Susan told me she had never, ever felt so utterly alone as she had then; standing in the Lord's house pleading to Him and to a Christian Brother, just for someone to hug her and to show her some care. She said the chasm between us was immeasurable from where she stood, and although she claimed to have understood my campaign, and fully respected my decision, my dedication, and me; she felt she could not understand why The Almighty would allow her to suffer in such a miserable and lonesome way.

* * * * *

Autumn is often a time for accepting responsibility for our actions.

* * * * *

Susan said she felt isolated, alienated, and even alone at the supermarket surrounded by so many others. Other women, other white women, would give her dirty looks for having married a black man, even though Marvin was mostly dark brown.

I guess none of them had ever read the Song of Solomon, or all about how the lion would eventually lie down with the inevitable lamb…

* * * * *

October used to be the only month that could justify the use of the three-letter word "Boo."

* * * * *

We taped paper angels all over the walls. We placed little white candles on each of the tables. We tied wheat, bunches of sorghum wheat, to all of the posts, or used these bunches as centerpieces along with chrysanthemums and cornflower. By the time we were finished, the church looked more prepared for a wedding than for a Christian alternative to a Halloween party. The room was breathtaking.

We kept our eyes where they belonged.

* * * * *

We never really feel the chill, until November.

* * * * *

October 1st made me long tremendously for the first day of September; all was moving way too quickly from the start. I had not yet cut enough wood to get the church, the parsonage, and my cottage through the winter. There were still hundreds of things to get done before the first snow. Time was fleeting. I was shaking, yet God was still on my side.

On September 1st, I merely had an insignificant and innocent crush on a sweet, intelligent, young married woman named Susan – nothing too detrimental, not even a sin – not a sin because I hadn't once dreamt of acting upon my feelings. By November 1st though, to my dismay, I began to hope her husband might perish tragically, leaving her to me.

The only problem was; I actually liked Marvin. I also enjoyed working with him, for the most part, and those odd particulars made me feel like a dirty heel. This made it even more so disturbing to wish him dead. Like I said, I liked him, problem was though; I could not respect him, and that little flaw is what opened the door to the sin of wanting to replace him forever in their bed.

Marvin may have been an adulterer, but in my heart, once or twice every day and every evening, I dabbled in thoughts that ran treacherously close to breaking the sixth commandment. There is adultery, and then there is murder. It is strange how God has placed them, so closely together on that list…

* * * * *

October is the time of year when we move our fires inside.

* * * * *

Marvin Watts and I had been chopping wood for many hours at the edge of the forest before I finally let go of wanting to strike him with my axe. I gave my anger and lack of compassion over to Jesus Christ; I stood upright, and then wiped my brow and let out a very deep sigh. Mentally, I was searching the scriptures for somewhere brotherly to begin, some place full of both the wisdom of Solomon and the lessons of the Master.

If I were to cross that bridge by bringing up the subject of my assistant's infidelity, I knew I would have to do it in a way that did not sound judgmental. Most of all, as a Christian Brother; I could only do it if I were to do it out of love. The most difficult part was in differentiating between my Christian love for Marvin, and my often blurry, confusion filled love for his lovely, Christian wife.

I held on to my axe and took some time to think things over while Marvin carried yet another split log over to the growing pile.

* * * * *

Hold onto September days for as long as you can; they are not cheap, and they do not come easy.

* * * * *

I stood with my gloved hands balanced atop my axe's long handle, resting easily on the smooth oaken tip. My breath white in the November air, I could no longer comprehend my true intentions. I could no longer tell what sort of creature I had become, that is, until I looked over at Marvin and noticed that his breath was white too.

"Marvin…"

"Yeah, Boss?"

Marvin stopped after placing another log section vertically upon the chopping block, and then he too took off his gloves and rested.

I looked at his leg first, and then up to his neck, wondering if a disabling shot would be the best of first choices, rather than to miss the completion of a deadly first blow and risk the discovery of what I may have become then. I listened to the woods all around us. Not a sound. Yet I could feel the beating of my heart within my chest, and I hated the man I was and what I might by the end of that day, become.

Marvin rarely attended church, but he professed Christianity. Saved? I do not know and did not know it then. If he was saved, and I were to kill him; he would go straight to heaven, for that I was sure. There was only the case of the adultery for which he would still have to repent before death lest he risk it all on that favor. Forgiven? I do not know. God says He forgives us *if* we repent for each one of our sins.

For a moment, I dared to wonder just what becomes of a man that dies so suddenly he does not have the opportunity to repent.

Who could say anything about Marvin? I could not even figure out me.

Jesus tells us we must ask for forgiveness first. The gift of salvation is conditional. We must ask for it wholeheartedly, and humbly, and then we shall receive. That is what the book says He says, anyway.

Would I have taken Marvin's chance to ask for forgiveness away by killing him quickly? That was the question… after all, who was I to judge him in that critical moment, and beyond that; how burdensome a sin is it to rob a man of his last chance at redemption?

With that axe in my hand, who was I to judge *him*? As a

Christian man, why was I even having such thoughts?

* * * * *

Autumn, with its visibly lower, even softer auburn sunsets, is like the tender first dream of a newly born child. Autumn, with its fiery woods, its colorful leaves all aglow, is like a campfire frozen in time. Autumn, with its offerings of mercy, and it's even deeper understanding of this life and death on Earth, is a worthy companion so few of us turn to for comfort and relief.

Autumn can be a healthy time for repentance and atonement, whereas winter comes on colder, more desperately, even harsher, like a deathbed confession spoken all alone in the dark.

* * * * *

I just stared at him as he placed his gloves down upon the chopping block, trying hard to have compassion for this man within my heart of Christian hearts. Could I call myself a Christian any longer? I could not rightly tell – every man has thoughts, they say – where does the sin begin?

Does it begin with the thought? Does it begin in the heart? Would the sin have only begun if I were to have raised my axe and taken a step towards him? Would it all have hinged upon whether I chose to pick up the axe?

When does the sin begin?

Knowing then that I was not a 'good' Christian, if I ever had been, well; there I was, desperately in need of Christ's assistance, and trying my best to remain as Christian a man as I could be. I found myself planning Marvin's murder out there in those woods.

I would not use the axe, I just knew that, but by day's end, I sincerely wanted nothing more than to spiritually slay him and leave him to rot.

Is that a sin? I wondered.

*　*　*　*　*

Autumn is a time for deep reflection: Water, water, mirrored mare, what monster's face, beneath my hair...

*　*　*　*　*

"What's on your mind, Boss? Hey, you mind if I get one of those smokes?"

Marvin knew how to ask for a favor.

*　*　*　*　*

In mid September, you can watch as the last of the twisted, distorted, cold weather flowers die off slowly, browning, while the sweet scent of new firewood and freshly cut kindling mixes with the scent of autumn's freshly fallen leaves.

We had a small brush fire going, the sweet smell of smoke; just a little burn pile to do away with our cleanup from the churchyard. We had coveralls, our gloves, our boots on and our parkas. There was plenty of scenery cut by crisp blue. There was also a very cool breeze blowing. The steeple set against the bright blue sky, the damp and grey looking stones of the graveyard with their chiseled, ancient writing under the great shadows of the trees, the neighboring farm... all these things and more, as a backdrop to his death.

Mulley Creek was running clearly and nicely due to all the recent rain, yet there was also something else. There was another something not quite as tangible as all the other things in the air, yet dutifully present, and present within me.

"Whenever two or more are gathered in His name."

There was no way I could ever have killed him, yet I wanted to, sincerely.

*　*　*　*　*

Autumn is a time for taking caution near thin ice, although it usually does not appear before November.

December second is the perfect time to watch the stars above.

* * * * *

"What's that, Boss?"

All I could think about were Susan's eyes; I hated that about Marvin's presence, and I hated that about myself. I truly hated that then.

I cleared my throat and answered Marvin, "I said, 'When two or more are gathered in His name.'"

Marvin laughed, "Praise the Lord, Boss. Praise Jesus. Can I get one of them smokes now?" He was laughing.

I handed Susan's husband a smoke.

"Thanks Boss, and thank you too, Mr. Man-upstairs!" and he pointed the cigarette up toward the sky, "Thank you too, as well, for this here blessing."

I could not hate him, no matter how hard I tried, and when I did feel something awful? Well, I simply refused to act upon it. That is how I managed to stay out of prison that year, and out of Hell.

* * * * *

December second is the perfect time to see a shooting star. It will plant your feet in the snow and send you soaring.

* * * * *

Marvin had a terrific, if not disarmingly friendly smile. He had nearly perfect white teeth, set well into his solid jaw, his smoothly polished skin. Susan had revealed to me that this attribute of Marvin's, as she put it, "His warm and welcoming, bright and reassuring smile," was the thing that first attracted her to him. I could not deny this: the man certainly possessed a subtle, if not outwardly gaining charm.

He could have operated a circus tent in Hades. He could have sold most anyone most anything at all. I thought he had missed his calling; he should have been in sales, but instead he stole Susan's heart while she was still in her college years, while desperate, and now he had her, and he was doing what he wanted.

They used to park by that old gray bridge over Mulley Creek every Friday afternoon.

* * * * *

Autumn can be a most desperate time when it comes to falling in love.

* * * * *

Marvin was inspecting the dominant focus of my indecision curiously, smoking his cigarette with malice and with the aid of that devilish smile, with suspicions of me. I could clearly tell what was on his mind. He hid all those pearly white teeth as he watched me tinker with my inconclusiveness.

Meanwhile, I was toying with the serpent as I stood, trying desperately to hide within the shadow of the cross.

"So, what's on your mind, Boss?" He said to me, "You look uneasy," and he stretched out the word 'easy' as if to let me know he knew.

I knew that he knew what I was thinking, and I guessed then that the spirit was telling him, and me, that he knew what it was that I knew then.

Marvin's eyes looked down, and then he shattered me with his utterance, "Ain't no thing but a chicken wing, Boss... I'm just being a man, that's all – the proverbial sinner, you could say – ain't no thing, no thing at all, really." Then he finished his smoke and put his gloves back on.

* * * * *

Autumn can be terribly cold and cruel for some, cold, cruel, and disheartening. It can be a lot like that very first bite of cat food as it rests on the end of the fork, when you are elderly

91

and poor.

*   *   *   *   *

"Why is the sky blue, Susan?"

"Because God made it that way," and she giggled.

"No, seriously. I know God made it that way, but *why* is it blue?"

"Because it's sad?"

I laughed. I had to. Then I laughed again. Her pleasantries were contagious.

"No, seriously, and no offense intended, but, do you know the real answer?"

"Maybe…"

"Susan..." and I took it slowly, "I know you are an intelligent young woman, and I respect your mind, but I want to know if you really know the scientific answer."

"Does anyone really know the answer to that question?"

"I do."

"O.K." and she paused delightfully, semi-securely, "Then go ahead. Tell me. Tell me why the sky is blue."

"It…" and I had to make sure I was about to do this thing correctly, "It has to do with sunlight, and rainbows, and nitrogen, and how sunlight behaves when it strikes nitrogen atoms, and also it has to do with how we look up at it: our perspective on it. Are you sure you're ready to hear this? The last thing I want to do is to bore you."

I did not want to bore her ever. After all, it was the first week of September. We were now friends. It was all about conversation and connecting verbally, and nothing at all about love. Nothing like that at all.

"You're not boring me, go on."

"O.K."

"O.K."

"Aright then, the sky is blue because of this…"

*   *   *   *   *

92

Autumn is the time of belly up dead crickets in our pathways, luxurious baths, cinnamon toast, truffles, fleeting dreams of consummation while being serenaded by a dream within a dream. Autumn is a time for romantic impulses. Autumn is a time for spirits and for minds to share what many do not dare. Autumn is the funerary pyre for all the dying fireflies.

Autumn is a time for breaking from the sandy, stony bottom of the shallows and daring to swim away out toward the deep.

* * * * *

Her eyes were like two blue comets that would not fade away in daylight. I had always believed that they were eyes that would not ever dare to fade. Susan's eyes were like that for all the many days that I knew her; like beacons, like two patches of blue sky beckoning me to soar.

"O.K., it's like this: the sky, our sky," I was excited to share it with her, "is like a rainbow that can only show you the color blue. Am I clear?"

"Are you what?"

"Clear."

"Clear?"

"Clear."

"What?"

"Do you understand what I am saying?"

"Nope."

"Try this on for size…"

Susan was staring at me oddly and I could not tell why or what it was she was thinking at that moment. I liked to think that she was impressed, enamored, entertained, bewildered, enthralled… captivated by the random strangeness of my inquiry, yet mystified by the depths I would endeavor to explore with her. Yes, all those big and beautiful words; I wish they had all applied to me back then.

Unfortunately, it was simply that Susan, although educated in many senses, had never really taken any interest in the sciences, and so was lost in the conversation.

"You know how a rainbow shows you the seven colors concealed within white light?"

"Yeah, ROY. G. BIV. The rainbow. I get that much."

"Well, just like the spray of a hose can show you a rainbow; the sky, our sky, is a rainbow or, well, more like a prism, although rainbow does work, that only reveals, or isolates, and shows us the color blue."

Susan went still and quiet.

"And because our atmosphere is shaped the way it is, in a sphere, and because it is comprised of 78% nitrogen, which tends to scatter blue light, well, when you look up, the sky appears to be blue."

Susan looked quizzical, "Appears blue? I thought the sky is blue?"

"Nope. Sorry. The sky is clear. It only appears blue. It is a rainbow during the day that can only show us the color blue. If it were truly blue, well, then the Moon and stars would have to be blue at night. Right?"

"You're kidding," and she took a moment to look up at the sky.

"Nope. The sky is only blue during the day."

Susan was still looking up at the sky while I dreamt of kissing her.

*   *   *   *   *

Autumn often remains silent, even when it has a lot to say.

*   *   *   *   *

Marvin's countenance was just a little more than I could stand, even with his cocky smile – that smile that only moments before his statement to me was so warm and friendly – and it was too much for me to remain comfortable with, in silence. The smell of freshly chopped wood and autumn's smoke still filled the air.

"So what's up, Boss?"

"How can you…" I felt beleaguered, "How can you do what

94

you are doing to her?"

He was laughing again, directly at me this time, while generously sharing that smile of his.

"Hey…" he said casually, as if he was trying to ward me off in the friendliest of fashions.

"Seriously, Marvin, how can you cheat on Susan like this?" Not, *"How can you cheat on your wife, like this?"* No, at that moment she was purely Susan with regard to the enemy, and to me.

* * * * *

Springtime makes us feel larger. Summertime makes us feel small. Autumn has a very big way of making us feel even smaller, preciously smaller in so many ways.

* * * * *

"You got a thing for Susan, don't cha Boss?" and he laughed at me again. "Everyone does… at first."

* * * * *

Autumn has a way of making us feel smaller, as if we are shrinking, growing tinier in space and time as we grow older and learn so much more and more. We learn, and with each lesson, learning only how little it is we really know for sure.

* * * * *

"No."

That is what I said, and that is how I said it, but the truth was I wanted everything for her, and I wanted her, and I could not stand that he was talking about her the way he was, and that he had her for his own.

"No, I don't," and I continued to lie, "I just don't understand why a man like you would treat her that way."

"A man like me?" Marvin put his axe down. His breath

growing whiter as it mixed with the cold air before him. The white was billowing out from his lungs as he spoke to me. He was visibly angered, yet holding it back, courageously, "Why? Because she's *white*? Shit, Boss, fact is, she probably likes it. Bible says it – they were made for our pleasure – they were made to please us, that's why they are here in the first place, Man. Been that way ever since Adam and Eve. Shit... you know that."

He was shaking his head back and forth, tugging at the base of his gloves, picking up his axe once again.

* * * * *

Autumn is a time in which we teach the boys to do the killing. Someone always has to be the one to swing the handle that leads to the blade, down upon the throat of our future, upon the neck of our sacrifice, for the purpose of our survival.

* * * * *

I could hardly take it any longer, but then again, I had to.
Praise the Lord.
"You give me all the keys and blessings with which to satisfy my artful curiosity, Lord. I love you, I love you, I love you. Now please, fortify my strength – dear sweet Jesus – for I am about to do battle with Satan himself and I am afraid that I might kill."

* * * * *

Susan tacked another paper angel to the wall. It was a handmade angel, made by her two precious hands. The children made some of the other paper angels. Never before had I seen an effort displayed with such gentle and caring grace afforded. I stood on the ladder and watched, amazed.

Susan was gorgeous. A temptation lay before me, or a lesson, I could hardly tell.

* * * * *

Autumn… sweet Jesus, help me. Help your servant please.

* * * * *

"So that's it? That's how you really feel?"
"The Lord forgives me, so what do I care what other people think?"
"Just like that?"
He seemed so confident.
"No repentance… no, *'Sin no more?'* "
I smiled for what felt like the first time in eons.
Marvin looked at me oddly, "What's all that?"

* * * * *

Autumn can slap us silly when her sweet coloration catches us even partly off-guard.

* * * * *

"Boss," and he was laughing lightly, but not so eerily cool as with before, "If I didn't know any better, I'd swear you was sweet on my wife." He was eyeing me more closely then, "Yeah, that shit will pull you in a thousand ways. Yeah, Boss, you oughta get yourself a woman of your own before you go talkin' to me about covortin' and such." And he laughed even harder, "Man, you serious? You don't even know the way things are and you're judging me?"
I could have run up and punched him then, but he was right. I could have cut him down with my axe, but I was concerned for my soul, and worst of all, he was right. Not rightly justified in cheating, but he was correct in his assumption regarding my feelings for Susan. It did not feel good to be in that position at all. In addition, he was correct in the fact that I was judging him.
"You're serious?" and now he was really laughing.

I could have struck him in the leg and then finished him off on the ground. I could have struck him in the head and left him there to bleed out while I walked away and wasted time elsewhere. I could have made it look like it was an accident. I could have beaten the rap… there were enough men in town to guarantee me a jury of *their* peers.

"Boss… you?"

I could have killed him and buried him. I even thought about how I could dig his grave beneath the fire ring where we burned all the rubbish, and how I could make the grave disappear by simply burning enough branches and leaves to make the ground look as if it had been that way for centuries. How no one would probably look for him anyway with the way things were in town, but damn it all to hell, I loved her, and if she truly loved him I could not do that to her. Besides, I did actually like him, despite my distaste for his deeds and actions.

Susan was a Christian woman, and for me to kill her husband would mean that I would have to lie to her about his murder for all of eternity, and I could not have that thing between us. Plus, the truth was, she really did love him, so there I was…

* * * * *

By day, autumn can appear to be never ending.

* * * * *

Movement and repose, movement and repose; that is what separates us from the dead, movement and repose. That, and hand me down thoughts; hand me down dreams and clothing.

* * * * *

Two by two they meet,
two by two they dance,
and two by two sweet autumn's Moon

puts them in a trance.
Two by two we enter,
but one by one we leave,
between the start and stop of things,
be ever mindful of what you believe.

* * * * *

His attitude was so wicked I began to estimate how long it would have taken for me to dig that hole beneath the burn pile.

* * * * *

Autumn is an ember slowly burning into the night.

* * * * *

We finished stacking the woodpile, at least for that afternoon, in relative silence. Forty cords in all, thus far.

September had been a rainy month, the creek was high as a testimony to that spell of weather, and the leaves had been rich in color, holding fast, as rain will make them do. However, October came on wearily from the very beginning; damp, cold, foggy, as if in a perpetual state of saturation. The bark of every tree looked black. By October 5th, I think maybe half the town had forgotten what a blue sky even looked like.

Autumn and death can be like that: they can remove things from our sight.

* * * * *

Autumn, like some malicious magician, causes the color green to slip away and disappear.

* * * * *

As Marvin drove off that day, I stood by the rectory door praying silently for forgiveness. I prayed silent prayers of thanks, and prayers of protection. Some were prayers of love; how much I love God. There were prayers for my family mixed in there too, a few prayers for Susan, and then I prayed for her husband's salvation as well.

* * * * *

Autumn will always be a time for second chances.

* * * * *

Many, many things drive me to communicate with God. When I was a child, it was mostly fear that drove me into His presence. Often, it was the fear of punishment at the hands of my parents that inspired me. I would plead with God, and I would beg God to fix the broken window, beg God to keep my father's anger small, beg God that my mother would not kill me for something I had done. Later, I would ask God for things, selfish things; please let me win the lottery, please get her to like me, please let me do well on this exam that I did not study for. Please make me taller and more handsome; please do not let grandma and my new pet goldfish die…

As I grew older, there were times when I would talk to God and beg Him to change the world and to make it a better place to live in. I would pray for safety when I would wander. I would ask for answers. I would pray for peace. I would pray for the men and women at war.

When Jesus finally saved me in my mid-twenties, I acknowledged my sin and repented… and I asked for forgiveness. It was then that I began to pray for the souls of others in an entirely different way.

You see, I never hated Marvin. Yes, there were times when his behavior angered me, and yes, the worldly man inside of me wanted to correct him, punish him, even kill him for all he had done to Susan, but I knew that was God's responsibility and God's job alone. Moreover, because Susan had chosen him as her mate, and because she loved him, I could not truly hate him or allow myself to harm him in any way. Why? Well, it is because I love the Lord, because I loved Susan as well, and so, by default, I had to love and accept Marvin as a brother, as well.

Actually, as a Christian, it was my duty to love him either way.

* * * * *

Autumn brings the lonesome cricket to your doorway or window, to play his lonesome solo for you just before dinner or bed.

Autumn is a steep reminder that you are not alone.

* * * * *

I ate my supper all by myself that night as I most often did back then. Outside my window, one lone cricket chirped away as October's darkness crept into the yard, winding its way around the chimney top, dragging my home toward Halloween. I had a small pumpkin on the windowsill, one I had grown in the rectory garden. It was a deep yellow-orange. Looking at it made my heart ache to see the color blue in the sky once again.

* * * * *

Autumn is a reminder to us all, to slow it down.

* * * * *

While hanging decorations in the church, Susan had asked me if I still had any dreams left that had not yet come true.

* * * * *

Autumn can be as riveting as it can be devastating.

* * * * *

I did not know how to answer her right then.

* * * * *

Autumn causes us to pause, that is, if we are listening to her right. Otherwise, you may just turn away and simply continue.

* * * * *

I did have dreams once. In high school I dreamt of going to college, and I did go, but not for very long. I got an associate's degree, ran out of money, took my job as a landscaper with plans of saving money for school and re-attending. The year was 1965. There were rumors of war. Things got strange; I took some time off and dabbled in pretending to be a hippy, and then I rediscovered God and moved back home.

Dreams? I had them every evening. Some better, some bad. But real dreams? Aspirations? Lofty goals and great desires? I could no longer rightly tell. I longed to see the giant redwoods out in California. I wanted to see Niagara Falls. I still hoped to see the Grand Canyon, possibly even visit the ocean again someday.

How far away was I from home?
Where is home?

* * * * *

Winter is the only season that happens twice a year.

* * * * *

Dreams? I think I let them go every time I turned the news on. Just knowing Susan and Marvin was just about leveling me with the floor. Dreams? I dreamt daily about loving someone just like Susan. I dreamt of finding my way back home into the arms of a woman I could love.

I could not answer her just then, so I turned and walked away.

* * * * *

Autumn can be brilliantly illuminating.

* * * * *

Moments later, I turned to Susan and told her all about the things I really wanted to do. I told her about my desire to see the redwoods, Niagara Falls, the Grand Canyon, and we talked about creation and all the wonders of the world.

I told her I believed that evolution; *Creation with just a little more of God's orchestration*, was how God really made all things. She told me that was lovely, a lovely way of elucidating and expressing that. She said she would like to see the great wonders also. Maybe to walk along the great wall in China, maybe even one day get to see the Alps.

"I'd like the war to end though. I'd like to see all wars come to an end, forever."

Then we agreed that we shared common ground amidst that particular dream.

* * * * *

Autumn opens up the door to all our forgotten wishes and autumn reminds us all that we can in no way live our lives for someone else.

* * * * *

All I really ever wanted to do was to meet a good, Christian woman like Susan. She would not have to be perfect, although a perfect replica of Susan would have suited me just fine.

So why did God have to bring her into my life and have her be married to somebody else? That question nearly drove me insane for many horrible months.

Later on, I discovered that not everything is always about me.

*   *   *   *   *

October is reluctant to give up its reign over autumn. It holds on to its placement in time much in the way an oak tree holds on to its brown leaves. It argues for its limitations, begrudging November in a form of sibling rivalry matched by no other two.

*   *   *   *   *

The following day at work was not an easy one for me. I did not feel at all healthy being around Marvin Watts. I felt sickened physically, drained, annoyed, and achy, while Marvin appeared to be chipper and feeling just fine. I also felt spiritually weakened.

That is what happens when you hang around a sinning sinner; you experience death of the soul by proxy and it surely comes on fast.

*   *   *   *   *

Autumn takes its time in getting to where it is going. After all, who in their right mind would simply rush right into winter?

*   *   *   *   *

At noon the second day, after Susan and I had completed most of the decorating for the harvest party, we stepped outside after lunch for a much-needed cigarette. The autumn leaves were at their peak and colored to perfection, as it had been such a warm and wet year. Our Indian summer had lasted for what felt like nearly a month.

We walked through the cemetery and out towards the pond by the edge of the woods. We could smell autumn's fragrance blending with those of the dairy farm next-door, and in strange and familiar ways, it was exciting.

When we stopped at the pond's edge, Susan marveled at the

reflection of the yellow, orange, black, and red forest on the chilly water's surface. She had not yet been down to the church's pond before.

There were a few leaves floating on the water; smallish, jagged, quaking aspen leaves all dressed in yellow, along with the larger maple leaves painted mostly red.

Down by the water, Susan talked a little more about her daydreams, and she talked with me about how she often felt like just packing a bag and running away. She informed me that something felt very wrong inside of her and inside her home, and that lately Marvin would not even look at her when he came home from work on a Friday afternoon.

I wanted to tell her what I knew and all I had witnessed, but I could not bring myself to do this terrible thing.

She threw a stick out into the pond then, shattering the placidity of the forest's reflection in the way an abrupt sound can wrest you from a deep and comfortable sleep.

The stick made but a little audible sound as the water swallowed it whole within the breaking of its surface, but somehow it felt as if someone had shattered a very large mirror of glass.

* * * * *

October causes us to open up our lexicons, to dust off words like "Chilly" and "Responsibility" and to take them out and to use them more frequently than not.

* * * * *

As the ripples caused by the stick she had thrown made their way across the water's surface, Susan turned to me, coughed, and said, "What this pond needs is a boat."

"A boat?"

"Yeah, it's such a beautiful pond. It should have a boat, like a rowboat or a canoe."

I tried to imagine it.

"You think?"

The thought of placing a boat on its waters had never crossed my mind before. I had always fished from shore.

Susan took a few steps towards the pond with her arms lifting upward, as if she was about to adjust a picture frame on a wall. She then traced a very large rectangle in the air before her as she spoke, "I can't imagine a more beautiful pond..."

The water was almost as still then as it had been when we had first arrived.

"...but all we can do is stand here and look at it. If we had a boat, or a canoe, we could be part of the picture."

Hers was a very lovely thought.

"We could row out to the center, or travel all around the water's edge. In the spring we could look for turtles over there by that fallen tree, but without a boat, all we really get to do is stand here."

At that moment all I wanted to do was to row away with Susan forever. I could picture it. I could picture the two of us floating on the mirrored water, looking down at the reflection of the sky and the clouds above us. And how, if Marvin was gone, I could reach out and touch her hair...

* * * * *

Autumn is replete with great distractions.

* * * * *

Like the way spots of rain on concrete can tell you that the sky is about to begin falling, Susan peppered me with silence as we walked back through the gate in the cemetery wall. Having finished all her thoughts on boats, and dreams, and wishes, her demeanor had changed. She was pregnant with something she could not yet bring herself to speak of, and I prayed she would not bring up the subject of Marvin again.

Infidelity.

I often wonder. If she had asked me then, could I have lied to her or would I have spilled the proverbial beans?

Would I have had the right to do so?

* * * * *

Autumn brings back memories, like the way the mud and even the air around, can often reek of manure and milk well beyond the confines of a dairy farm. If you do not know that special flavor of breeze, you are missing out on something terribly.

* * * * *

We used to buy all of our milk from the dairy farm next door. The walk there and back took just a little over twenty minutes. We had to cross the bridge over Mulley Creek to get there. Crossing that bridge with Susan made me shiver the first time we did it together and then again from time to time. I used to tell myself that feeling helped keep the milk cold during the walk.

* * * * *

Autumn is the time for purple blossoms in the forests, upon the ironwood in fields.

* * * * *

On the way back from the pond's edge toward the cemetery, I picked a Queen Ann's lace flower and introduced Susan to the source of German purple.

* * * * *

Autumn is a time for new beginnings, for beginning something new.

* * * * *

Susan was unaware that German settlers had brought the Queen Ann's lace flower, the plant otherwise known as the wild carrot, here to America. It was and always has been their source of a dye for clothing. In the center of the broad, flat, white lacy blossom is a tiny flower with four petals, a miniscule structure that produces permanent violet dye. The flower generates this pigment for what reason, I do not know. I just know that it does. This small, organic, purple spec is the sole purpose for which they plant it. Sometimes it reminds me of a spider sitting in the middle of a web.

"The Amish dye their shirts and dresses with it."

"Funny. Looking at the flowers, I always thought that was a little bug."

* * * * *

Autumn is a time for brief reminders of the present.

* * * * *

After her moment of silence had passed her, Susan revealed to me that her favorite color was in fact purple, and she commented on how God's placement of the dye within the flower was nothing short of a tiny miracle. She also told me then that she wanted to spend her life working with children, and then she told me she was quite sure she was incapable of having children of her own.

Then, there within the cemetery walls amidst the fiery gravestones, Susan began to weep.

She cried a lot in front of me that year.

* * * * *

Autumn is a time for dewdrop lightening, cast upon the surface of summer's most delicate webs.

* * * * *

Then she started screaming…

* * * * *

The fallen leaves, they float downstream, over autumn's chilly beds.

* * * * *

Then she came at me. And then she pounded my chest with tears in her eyes until I had to take a step backwards in order to ward off her blows.

* * * * *

Autumn decays with her precious blooms so they might each bloom again someday.

* * * * *

To separate myself from her previously undeclared rage, I removed myself in a brisk retreat backwards, then stopped; destroyed altogether due to the fact that I could not hold her then to offer her some comfort during her time of magnificent release.

* * * * *

Autumn is the color of the great chasm between Heaven and Hell.

* * * * *

Marvin worked under me for exactly two months and three days before the church board decided to let him go. He did not work on Saturday, so Susan and I had the property to ourselves, but even so, I refrained from getting any closer.

We just stood there. Me, silently, she screaming and shouting out vile epithets, quite nearly cursing at God.

I wanted to touch her in an attempt to bring her back down

and to console her, but I could not trust myself to do so without longing in an invitational fashion, so I had to just let her go on screaming and shouting at the world.

It was then that I first got a glimpse into why she stayed with Marvin despite what her instincts were telling her. Due to her perceived inability to carry children, she had imagined that no other man would ever have her. So, she had decided to accept whatever Marvin chose to do, as long as he would continue to keep her.

She did not say this, but it was palpable in every one of her words.

* * * * *

Autumn is the time of year when even the silence seems to shout.

* * * * *

They fired Marvin three days after our Harvest Party for tossing a beer bottle out of his car window onto church property. It wasn't even the fact that he'd been drinking that brought it on. The person who saw him do it was himself a consumer at times, but he was mostly offended by the act of littering on church property, which he felt insulted both the church and God, along with the entire tithing congregation as well, and their children, and their ancestors buried on church grounds.

Marvin admitted to what he had done and even apologized for his actions, but still they let him go.

Later, he told all who would listen that they fired him because he was black.

* * * * *

Autumn lulls the woodland creatures, wooly, into slumber. Autumn reminds us all to prepare for the worst while enjoying the best. Autumn is life's retest for those who fail to wake up in the spring.

*   *   *   *   *

I cannot say I was overjoyed at the prospect of relinquishing my duties of overseeing and working alongside Marvin, but I did experience a sense of great relief no longer bearing witness to his illicit, creekside retreats. The loss of his job, and subsequently, his loss of an income just prior to the holidays, were hard on Susan. Even difficult for me, because I knew she had a lot on her plate.

What it did serve to do was to get Susan out of the house, taking a job as a classroom helper at the local elementary. She enjoyed that more than waitressing, which is what she had done at two locations before Marvin took the job with me.

At the elementary, she worked in the mornings and afternoons with the smallest children. Midday, she helped prepare their lunches. It was good for her, a dream come true, or so it seemed.

They say God never closes a door without first opening a window, or even still, another door. For Susan and me, Marvin's firing was a true blessing in disguise.

*   *   *   *   *

November can bring about two distinct changes in a person: One is that we dust off the snow shovel. Two, it reminds us we must soon buy a turkey. These are two distinct changes, but only one if you live in the South.

*   *   *   *   *

After a long, hot summer, and a very pleasant beginning to fall, November came on brutally, with our first measurable snowfall arriving on the eighth. No one ever prepares for an early snowfall in November.

We received two and a half feet by the ninth. The year was 1973. I was 29 years old and counting. Not nearly enough wood was cut to get the church, the pastor's residence, and my cottage through the entirety of winter. Now with Marvin gone, it would be up to me to cut it all on my own in the snow.

* * * * *

Autumn lasts well into December. Most people always forget that fact, year after year after year.

* * * * *

Our church was a very old building, and although we owned many acres of land and were not struggling as a congregation, no one had ever decided to change the furnace over to anything more modern than wood and coal generated heat. Stoking the furnace was laborious, yet job security for a good back like mine, and there was I, gloves on.

Two and a half feet of snow is a lot of snow, especially when you have not shoveled the white stuff in almost a year. I broke the handle of my shovel and had to replace it with another. I thanked God for giving me the good sense to keep around a few spares.

Everything in town shut down that day, everything except for Susan's pain and suffering. Marvin did not come home that evening. He blamed it on the snow.

* * * * *

Autumn can change a person's outlook on forever.

* * * * *

No one was in the church when I walked out to shovel the snow from the sidewalks by the entrance. Our pastor was out on visitation, checking in on some of our older members, making sure they had sufficient heat.

Later, coming up from the basement after stoking the furnace and reloading the wood rings by the fireplace in the

112

foyer, I noticed a lone silhouette in the sanctuary. The room was barely candle lit, and this figure was on her knees at the altar, apparently praying aloud.

* * * * *

November's logo is a tree stump, her favorite color ashen grey.

* * * * *

Usually, when someone entered the sanctuary all alone to speak with Jesus, our Father, or the Holy Spirit, I'd simply go about my business, allowing him or her to be. On that snowy November day though, I got curious, so I stepped outside to see whose car was in the yard.

* * * * *

A snowy autumn day affords a person a great opportunity to look up at the opaque and glowing grey sky to watch as the snow seemingly falls in endless approach. It is a perfect opportunity to experience one of God's simple blessings. The snow may kiss your face, your eyelashes, and all at once, you begin to notice how much sparkling color the sky truly holds when it is snowing. You can watch this all until the snowfall appears to turn blue as you look up.

* * * * *

Susan's car was in the driveway. This came as no surprise to me.

* * * * *

There is more than one reason why people term autumn, "The Fall."

* * * * *

Normally I would never listen in on a person's private conversation with the Lord, but there was already a foot of snow on the ground, and Susan had driven through it just to get to the church, and that one fact had me concerned.

She stayed and prayed for nearly four hours, and while she prayed, I kept her car mostly free of snow.

By the time she was finished speaking with God about her problems, her sincere desire to bear children, and her even stronger desire to see her husband reach salvation; she came and found me in the basement by the furnace, where I needed to be, and there she expressed to me her desire to embrace.

All she wanted was to hug me, but even still, I told her no.

"Why?" and she had tears on her face, the remainders of her prayer.

"Because it would be improper, that's why. The Bible tells us to refrain from even the impression of impropriety. We cannot touch. It would be wrong. I am sorry, Susan, but that is the way it is."

She was literally crying there in front of the furnace, "But how can it be wrong? I love you... you love me... you're..."

That was the first time Susan ever used those words towards me.

"You're my friend, John, and you're my Brother in Christ for Christ's sake. Please, you are the only one that really understands me and I cannot see why God would want us to grow so close and yet force us to stand so far apart. It's crazy!" just then she stomped her foot, "John, I feel like I am dying over here and all I want is for you to hold me, just once."

She choked up a little more. I did not know what to do then as my emotions and my logic were tearing me in one too many directions.

"It's like we're two feet away from each other and miles apart and I don't understand any of this at all. This - not being able to hug you when I need you - part of our relationship... it's even worse than waiting for Marvin to come home at

114

night. It is Hell, John, Hell, and I can't take it anymore. Oh, Jesus…" and she was looking up at the ceiling while tears streamed down the sides of her face in the flicker of the firelight, "God! Why can't I love this man and hold him? Why! Why!"

She was literally shaking in the shadowy glow.

"Why!"

So there it was.

"I love you! Don't you understand that?" she was looking directly at me.

It was out there on the table.

"Why won't you hold me?"

There we were in that old stone basement, warmed by the fiery furnace, and although it sounded like Heaven for a man who wanted nothing more than to be alone with a women such as she, I felt only inches from the searing fires of Hell. Anything could have gone wrong then. Anything.

* * * * *

November scares the wits from the young, but it scares the Hell out of those that fear growing old. It makes us want to race back to the Septembers of our youth, to a younger season some would sell their souls for the chance to embrace.

* * * * *

I had no idea how strong I really was until that day.

* * * * *

Autumn is nature's fire slowly dying out. Winter is life's pond freezing over, preserving within it the promise of spring.

* * * * *

Susan's hair was a little messy due to the snow and all of her crying. The melted snow had stained the shoulders of her sweater. My boots were still cold from working outside: this much I do remember.

She was wearing one of the sweaters she always looked so good in, and she had just said aloud that she loved me, and had admitted she had wanted to hold me, and that she needed me too. For a young man, this was temptation at its worst, and I have to admit I felt a bit hollow and shallow for feeling the things I had felt then, but I am only a man.

The best thing I could do, and I knew this, was to try my best to keep my distance. If we did not touch, we would both remain innocent of any wrongdoing. That was all I ever really knew... because one thing leads to another.

I could feel the furnace warming my flannel and baking the front of my jeans. My loins were burning. My legs were becoming even hotter. Susan went on pleading with me and with God above us. She was going on and on about how no one would ever know – how it was all so very innocent – and how there was absolutely nothing wrong with us hugging, simply hugging for comfort within the confines of the church for no other reason but love...

"It's all for love... love and for comfort and nothing more, John. I need you."

"But it could escalate."

"Escalate?" and she looked astonished, flabbergasted even. I feared I had overstepped an unseen boundary then, and perhaps that it was only I who had been having alternative thoughts. I panicked. She seemed fearless, undaunted by anything other than her quest to be loved.

"*Escalate?*" and she looked up at the ceiling and began laughing through her tears, "I hope it does escalate!"

I could not believe what I was hearing, but then again, I could. In that moment, my mind did the math and suddenly I realized that there was no possibility, aside from some queer act of God, that anyone should find us in that basement there alone. There was no chance that anyone else would ever come anywhere near the church that day due to the severity of the weather. No one, aside from Susan and our pastor, would even dare leave home in such a snow. The pastor's house was clear

116

across the property; nearly three hundred yards away, and pastor would certainly go directly home after his visitations.

Safely hidden within the confines of the basement of the church, it was true we could have gotten away with anything. There were the thick stone walls nearly one hundred years old and then there was all that earth and the naked roots of the trees to protect us. All that frozen ground.

Swallowed up in the belly of the sanctuary, in almost complete darkness aside from the glow of the fire, protected we were from above by the thick and ancient rough-hewn hemlock beams and floorboards also. Distance and a blanket of snow concealed us. Most of all, no one else ever entered the basement, no one, not ever, not even pastor. Most of the congregation was not even aware that it even existed below.

No one would have ever known what might have transpired there, no one, no one except for Susan and me, and no one else aside from God.

* * * * *

November has a way of making one feel as if it is their last day on Earth, how one might never again get the chance to perform the acts of their...

* * * * *

Susan moved in closer.

* * * * *

November's snow is chilly, whereas December's snow is mighty cold.

* * * * *

The firelight made her face look even more so beautiful than any light of day. I had not seen her lit so well in all the short time I had known her, and I felt weak in her presence. As if lit

117

just for me by firelight, this image of her was enough to get me to give in and float downstream on the winds upon which caution might be thrown. I wanted to give in. I wanted so much to simply let go... to give in completely to the freefall of sultry desire.

* * * * *

Never is a tree as vulnerably stark and bereft of any measure of defense as when lit by the dwindling twilight of a softly darkening November eve.

* * * * *

"Escalate?" Her words still carried in my ears, *"I hope it does escalate!"*

* * * * *

Never is a leaf as free as when lifted and carried upon the rising, then softly dwindling breeze.

* * * * *

There was no room left for me to back up in the basement. The wall was right behind me.

* * * * *

We must surely count the sunny days of November as rare jewels within autumn's silver crown.

* * * * *

I was cornered, yet I did not mind. Susan's curly hair was wet, back lit, and glistening in the light of the furnace glow before me.

*　*　*　*　*

Autumn can make seclusion feel so much more privately secured.

*　*　*　*　*

It was terrible, but in a strange, dark, and sinful way, it was completely thrilling and sexy, and there was something so ultimately wrong about it all that I very much liked that 'all alone' feel.

*　*　*　*　*

Autumn is a game of hide-and-go-seek within our pretense.

*　*　*　*　*

Split logs and lumps of coal were crackling in the furnace behind her. I had never felt so warmed before in all my life.

*　*　*　*　*

Autumn hides her crimson berries just beneath the cover of snow.

*　*　*　*　*

First, she looked down at the dusty, earthen floor, and then she looked back up to me, "I don't think you understand just how much I need you to love me right now, John. It's just a hug…" and she looked to her side as if someone was drawing her attention away then. "I am not asking you to sleep with me." Then she shook her head, "All I want is for you to hold me like a friend and a Brother. Just hold me. Just love me until this sick and horrible poison, this feeling of death gets out of me, out of my soul, so I can toss it into the fire and get rid of it all just for one day. Please!"

119

Good.

But not good enough…

"I can't touch you Susan." The small distance between us was charged.

"Why?" She whispered this in the wavering darkness closest to the wall.

"Because you are married," I whispered back sternly. It was painful.

That is when Susan pierced my soul. With her eyes, through the windows of my eyes, and through the doorways of my mind, with a venomous glare I do not ever wish to see repeated. Then she stabbed me through the heart and through the ears with her broadcast blows, words seething with reproach and hatred for all of man, myself included, "I saw them, John!"

I had to swallow hard then.

"I saw them and I know you know!"

* * * * *

There is nothing so quietly deafening as the silence of autumn's first snow.

* * * * *

"I saw them!"

I was a frozen man before that fire, leaning back against the wall.

"And I know you know!"

* * * * *

November wears a shade of grey that could scare a rabid squirrel.

* * * * *

I knew I was in love with Susan Watts the moment she first

began to speak to me at the gathering at our church barely three months before. It was about 5:30 on a Friday afternoon, August 28, 1973. What I did not know until November 8th of that very same year though, was that Susan was in love with me too. Either that or she was simply angry with her cheating husband and was willing to use me in order to get back at him. Either way, I felt enticed to oblige her, physically. I was spiritually lost and downtrodden.

It felt like a war was waging inside me.

War.

* * * * *

November's song contains verses forged from split wood and heated iron as it cries from deep within the coolness of the forest floor. Her strings are dried grasses wavering in the sunshine, her winds are the winds, her bass is the shade, and her crescendo is a thousand moonlit violins as they lie down upon the snow and lull to slumber.

* * * * *

"I'm not asking you to sleep with me; I just want you to hold me..."

Maybe this was a good thing: she was not there to throw herself at me, or so she said, she just *wanted* to throw herself at me. Maybe not even in a lustful way, maybe not in a sinful way. This was a spiritually and emotionally broken, desperate, recently rejected, and betrayed young woman that loved me, one who simply needed someone she cared about to hold her, and to hold her in the basement of the church by firelight where no one else could see and no one else would ever know. What could be more innocent than that?

Bullshit.

Although I sincerely loved and trusted her, I wasn't buying that.

Bullshit.

We would not have lasted in each other's arms for more than

121

two seconds without kissing hungrily, if not just to chase the memory of Marvin's indiscretion out of the way.

Horseshit.

So what was I to do?

* * * * *

Autumn is the friendliest of strangers bearing candy in a handmade basket; muffins, treats, and goodies all wrapped up in crimson and white and neatly tied up with a bow.

Banquet-like bouquets of brightly colored leaves and twigs, sprigs of juniper, boughs of pine... beware of any stranger bearing gifts.

* * * * *

I could not tell at first, there in the semisweet darkness, because the fire was behind her, but Susan had even more tears running down the sides of her cheeks. Then, before my eyes, this gentle young woman I had loved so terribly had transformed into a veritable chandelier of shimmering sadness, transfixed within the fire's light.

* * * * *

Susan began sobbing audibly, begging me with her pleas, reaching out to me with her arms, whispering painfully two words as she inched her way forward, "Please, John..."

I was absolutely confident that if I was to accept her into my arms that we would begin kissing, and then as sure as it would be wrong, and a sin, we would inevitably end up making love somewhere, if not right there in front of the furnace on some old woolen blanket on the floor. I could already taste the salty deliverance of her tearful languor, feel the chilly warmth of her face against my skin, and feel myself drinking in her teardrops as a child of sadness and desperation saps the nectar from a honeysuckle in spring.

I felt like a very bad man just then.

Yet, I could not imagine a more daring and romantic scenario - we could be together forever - Marvin's adultery would ensure an annulment, and Susan would then be free to remarry with anyone of her choosing. We could form the perfect union, Susan and I, and together we could start all over. Without Marvin's involvement, we could go anywhere together, go west and see God's magnificent canyons, walk hand in hand beneath the majestic redwood trees. We could be married *and* in love...

But I knew in my heart that if I were to walk her back to my cottage, arm in arm through the deepening snow, to build us a fire and then to take her, even save her, that our eternal, perfect union would be cursed and stained with sin. We would certainly pay for our indiscretion, even if it were to arise out of what we then perceived as necessity and need, out of human weakness, and we would pay for that sin for the rest of our lives.

"I'm not asking you to sleep with me; I just want you to hold me."

Bullshit, I was not about to take that fall.

* * * * *

November's stars appear to burn above the brightest.

* * * * *

I lowered my head and then glanced soulfully in Susan's direction without making contact with her eyes. I left behind the glow of the firelight and the furnace, walking up the cold stone stairs, alone.

* * * * *

Autumn can seal what feels like forever in a single drop of rain.

* * * * *

I did not look back down the stairs to see if she had followed.

* * * * *

November nights are the perfect nights to crack the windows open slightly before sleeping. The wealth of oxygen in the cool, rich air enhances all of our dreaming, and there is nothing more enticing than the act of snuggling into a freshly cooled bed in which to find our restful sleep.

* * * * *

Susan stayed in the basement and cried a tortured woman. I left the door at the top of the stairs cracked open for her return to the upper world of saints and humans. I could almost hear her heart breaking, and this hurt me, yet I knew what I was doing was right.

It killed me to leave her behind in the darkness, but I knew she would be warm down there, warmed by the hearth of the fire, and after all, she was in the Lord's home, and the choice I had made was far better than leaving her later, wrapped in a blanket of sin.

* * * * *

Autumn is the child that does not want to leave the park at sunset's closing.

* * * * *

While awaiting Susan's return to the sanctuary, I went over the facts of our existence in my mind.

Susan had apparently caught them in the act, or, at least that much I had assumed. Susan loved me, and I loved her more deeply than I had so far loved before. Adultery is the only legitimate, sanctioned reason for a divorce within Christianity. She had every right to leave him. She did not appreciate the way he treated her. I would marry her the day they got divorced.

These were the facts as they stood then. Unfortunately, I failed to include her potential for forgiveness in my brief and selfish account.

*   *   *   *   *

Autumn is to marriage as winter is to death.

*   *   *   *   *

"I love my husband, John. I don't want to leave him…" She almost found the notion humorous, "Is that what you thought I was suggesting down there? That you and I…"

She was hurt. In her mind, I had rejected her, yet she was pretending it wasn't that way at all.

I did not care what she was saying then, because fifteen minutes before, down there in the firelight, within the stone walls of the basement when it was her and I alone, there had existed the potential for her to allow for such comfort in my arms, and for us to be tempted. She had even said it aloud.

"Escalate? I hope it does escalate!"

So I wasn't dreaming.

"John… I love you, but I also love my husband. What I need from you is for you to be here when I need you, and to love me back. I need from you everything that Marvin will not…" and she looked around as if mice were scurrying around her feet and upon the floor, changing the direction of the subject then, abruptly, "I need you to support me as a Christian Brother, and as a friend. I am not a cheater. I could not do that. As a Christian, I would not do anything like that to seek comfort or revenge. That is not me and never was me. What I need is to know that I have someone I can trust, and that there is someone out there who cares, because, obviously, I cannot turn to my husband right now for that."

Bullshit.

"Then why me?" I have to admit I was angry for a few too

125

many reasons. "Why not turn to Jesus?"

Then she said this one thing that I have tried hard to, but have never been able to forget.

* * * * *

At times, autumn can be so very lovely that it may leave you speechless, terrifically secure, but just a little bit afraid.

* * * * *

There would be no divorce. Susan would seek no annulment. She would choose to turn her pain and anger over to Jesus, and to suffer diligently as Christ had chosen to suffer for us.

I, on the other hand, grew not only to respect her more for this decision than I had in all the days before that snowy evening, but also grew to hope that I would never have to look upon Marvin's dark visage again.

Low and behold, after forgiving him, Marvin began to attend church with Susan regularly, at least for some time and this fact drilled at me completely to the bone.

* * * * *

Autumn is an empty rowboat dancing close to shore.

* * * * *

Albeit forgiven, Marvin did not choose to discontinue his immoral affair. He just went on telling Susan that sinning is what sinners do and that was all.

* * * * *

November turns our thoughts to warm mugs any time of day, cupped appreciatively in both hands, as if we could somehow hold on to the fleeting temperature of the clay.

* * * * *

By the time we realized how long we had been talking, there was nearly three feet of snow on the ground. Susan's Chevy, the clunker she had borrowed from her cousin, slept quietly under a very deep blanket of snow. The laden white of November appeared impenetrable. Virginal, rounded, soft, and pleasing to the eye; every corner smoothed by the temperance of wind and white.

By the time we assessed all of this, it was nearly 5:30 in the evening, the snow was still falling steadily, although the flakes were now larger, and there was no possibility that Susan could manage to drive home.

She called Marvin. He told her to sleep at the church. He told her he did not feel like walking halfway across town to fetch her in the snow.

* * * * *

Each November morning grows colder than the one before, and then we simply get used to it. We stop complaining, stop shivering at every turn, and eventually we find ourselves looking forward to better days.

* * * * *

There was no way I could offer Susan a night in my cottage on the church property, even if she were to stay on the couch. I would have to try to get her home in my truck, but even that idea did not look promising.

We settled on calling the pastor and his wife shortly before dinner and they cheerfully agreed to take Susan in for the night. They kept two rooms dressed in the parsonage for just such charitable and often necessary occasions.

* * * * *

Autumn is that time of year when we must reacquaint

ourselves with gathering most happily at the table as a family or group.

* * * * *

We walked through the snow down the lane, which wound beyond the cemetery right to the pastor's front gate. The Sun had begun to set for our walk, and although dull and most certainly unimpressive, the way in which it shadowed the protruding tops of all the headstones made the place an awesome sight. The downy white snow was crisscrossed with tree branch fingerlings of shadowy blue, the pale, dim light of starlight essences. The rabbit tracks in the shallower drifts looked like Morse code messages sent through the cold.

As friends, we desperately wanted to hold hands for the walk. However, I would not do that to Marvin, and I would not insult God, and I would not insult my soul.

* * * * *

November mornings bring us gifts we should not refuse. They bring us the things that make us feel like little children once again, such as that endless train of icicles that used to form just above where you would walk outside, just above your front door, when you were younger.

November mornings can catch and hold the Sun for you within a single crystal of icy light.

* * * * *

Pastor's wife had been cooking a pot roast when we arrived at their door. She invited the both of us in with warm hugs and a generous smile.

The scents in the house were wonderful, and our dense and dire need for warmth and a dish of comfort food drew us to their hearth, their broad table, and to their company as well. Our hunger was satisfied, our shivers staved. In the food they shared with us, there was nourishment and fulfillment, and there was grace. There were potatoes, carrots, gravy, and wine, and the meat was delightfully fatty and tender, they way in which God intended all pot roasts to be.

* * * * *

November reminds us of the power of moonlight, the second light placed in the heavens to guide us on our way. The Moon is also there to remind us that we are never without God's light.

* * * * *

After a fine desert and coffee, I returned my hat to its proper place and headed out into the snow. On the way out the door, both pastor and his wife nodded knowingly to me, knowing I had done the right thing. I think it also had to do with how they each heard Susan thank me for my show of kindness, respect, and understanding in the undertaking of my duties as a Christian man.

My long walk home, which consisted mostly of retracing my former footsteps in the snow, began under the clearest of skies. Susan's undisturbed footsteps accompanied me all the way. The stars were all out dancing. The Moon was bright and near full. The shadows of the trees cast thinly, like mirrors of their upright and gentle makers, and everything in the world highlighted in white. Even the graveyard looked happy and content that evening. All that was left of the gravestones were strange white humps atop the deep snow.

The whole way back to the church, where I still had to stoke the fires before bedtime, all I could do was to smile and savor the sweet taste of Pastor's wife's apple pie and coffee, which so pleasantly remained on my palate.

On my walk from the church to my cottage, I could feel a little cool dampness entering into my boots. The feeling chilled me, causing me to pick up the pace.

I looked up to heaven and thanked God aloud for giving me the strength not to have opened the door to our possible sin.

No matter what she said afterwards, I know in my heart that I had truly done the right thing.

* * * * *

November is traditionally a time for expressing our thanks, for being altogether thankful, for getting down upon our knees and crying out in thanks.

* * * * *

The Christian alternative Halloween harvest party turned out to be a hit. Susan and I were each in attendance, of course, although Marvin did not come by.

* * * * *

October can be a time for both demons and angels. The ratio all depends on whom you invite to the party.

* * * * *

At the party, we bobbed for apples, drank copious amounts of delicious cider, sang songs together, and danced to music. There was even a harvest cake, a spice cake as I recall, adorned with vanilla icing.

Susan had done a fantastic job with the decorations, everyone said so, and all the other women had become inspired by her efforts.

Not one of the adults wore costumes. It was more a spiritual "Come as you are."

* * * * *

November is for the buttoning of sweaters.

* * * * *

I hung my wet pants by the door to my cottage in the mudroom on a peg, near to where I like to place my boots. I had to get the fire going in the stove because the fire had burned down to little more than a pile of warm embers by then. When it finally got to blazing, I closed the door, checked the venting, and crawled welcomingly into my bed.

That night I dreamt that Susan and I lived on a small boat that sailed upon the clouds within the heavens. It was just the two of us, accompanied by a whole host of various animals.

Dreams: chalk another one up for Noah, Daniel, and King Nebuchadnezzar.

* * * * *

November can find you standing alone in the darkness just about anywhere, wondering why everything feels so creepy while calling out, "Is anyone there?"

* * * * *

The snow did not hang around very long as the days that followed were nowhere near freezing. Everyone in town breathed a sigh of relief when it melted, but as soon as things were back to normal again we got another eighteen cold and lingering inches.

* * * * *

September is the month in which we pack our bathing suits away. In October, we get out our sweaters, but in November, at least in the North; we shop for long underwear and waterproof boots.

* * * * *

Forgiveness was never really a strong point of mine. In fact, as a child, I was the type that would hold onto grudges, and by child I mean until I was about twenty-five. In my walk with the Lord, I was working on that, yet I was nowhere near to where Susan's heart was in that capacity.

Susan had explained to me that what she saw that day regarding her husband's infidelity was Marvin driving with a woman (Teesha Daniels) in his car. She did not have to ask him, because as a woman, and as women often do, she just knew. She told me that the part that hurt her most was that the woman was the same race as Marvin: something that no matter how hard she tried, such a distinction was a thing with which she could never quite compete.

She sounded like a woman on a mission.

Susan's mother had told her that all men inevitably stray at some point or another, and that in the end; she hoped her forgiveness of him would heap coals of fire upon his head, and perhaps this act of mercy and kindness would lead him further toward repentance and salvation.

It was her only hope, her deepest need, and her wildest untamed dream. It was all so terribly sad that it would never quite happen that way.

* * * * *

November is the month in which many family members return to the place they once called their hometown for the purpose of gathering. It is a temporary, familial, annual migration hinged upon the yearnings of the heart and obligation. Sort of like the stalwart geese and the dainty Monarchs, the delicate emerald green hummingbirds, the mallards sharing colors of the same. The major difference is that people dress more amusingly than any one of these.

* * * * *

Susan was having a more difficult time struggling with the coming holidays than she would let on. For her, the coming holidays presented more of a challenge than the forgiveness of Marvin's transgressions. Sex, she said, was not very important to her. No, not as much as love and so infidelity was not as an explosive issue to her as it might be for those of us who place a far greater value and importance and emphasis upon it.

Maybe that is why infidelity has always been so infuriating to me?

The issue that was presenting greater difficulty to her was the fact that Thanksgiving was just around the corner, the fact that she had never fully recovered from the tragic loss of her mother, compounded by the fact that she had been excommunicated by what remained of her family for marrying a man of a different shade and color. The only one that would even talk to her was her cousin.

The holidays can be tough for some, but for Susan, the winter of 1973 would most closely resemble pure hell.

* * * * *

Autumn guides us to return to the very source of our understanding.

* * * * *

Susan survived Thanksgiving, but not without first breaking down. Marvin spent the holiday morning with Teesha Daniels, his girlfriend, after staying out the entire night before. This led to Susan burning her turkey, and by the afternoon; her mind, body, and spirit were in ruins.

Marvin still had not found a job to replace the one he had lost with me.

* * * * *

Autumn causes every leaf to fall, slowly, one by one, until autumn is finally over. In nature, rarely does anything occur without patience; not many things happen all at once. It is rare, but when this does happen, we refer to this as a catastrophe.

* * * * *

In the months that followed, I watched as Susan steadily began to lose weight. She began to appear under-rested and over-stressed most of the time, and then she looked unbearably thin. She had begun to pray with more fervor than anyone I had ever seen take to prayer for the salvation of another before.

Apparently, Marvin had taken his wife's forgiveness as permission to continue his illicit affair, and so rather than stop and repent for his actions and the harm that he was causing, he simply became a churchgoer for a month or two, and then even that adaptation came abruptly to an end. From what I could gather, he had since adopted Sunday morning as an addition to his Friday afternoon retreats, and he had begun this by staying out all Saturday night.

His behavior was all but killing his wife, but Marvin only ignored this.

* * * * *

Autumn can be a time for much recollection under authority, and it is a shame that oh so much can pass us by, as if we are blind.

* * * * *

Winter that year grew right out of fall the way a son comes forth from his father, meaning the apple did not fall very far from the tree.

It snowed six times during the cold month of November, leaving the floor of our world covered in white from the fifteenth onward. December was a slow month; slow in the sense that God had slowed us all down with his continuing abundance of frosty precipitation, and this reflected in our patience, and in all of our frustrations as well.

Since many people choose not to drive as much as they might otherwise when it snows, attendance was down at church for the rest of that year. The road, although plowed regularly, most often came across as lifeless, bleak, and barren.

The last true bit of life I can recall that autumn was one tremendous flock of Canada geese progressing in arrowhead fashion, directionally headed for the south, flying by in the grey overhead.

Susan was at prayer in the sanctuary almost daily after working with the little children at the school. Something told me she had already worn some calluses down on her knees.

* * * * *

Winter can often feel like a passage never ending.

* * * * *

By Christmas, I felt as if I could not take seeing Susan in such a terrible state anymore. She and Marvin were both living off her paltry salary from the elementary school, food stamps, and Marvin's far-from-ample unemployment check. It was barely enough for them to get by.

People whispered in the congregation about the fact that her clothing no longer fit her, and still others brought in dishes of food for her to take home. I gave her two hundred dollars right before Christmas, which was a large sum of money back then.

Susan cried when she opened the envelope, but she could not reject it. By then she had been far too humbled to rest any work of the Lord.

When Marvin discovered the money, he struck her and then he took what was left of it from her. Then he accused her of whoring around.

* * * * *

Wintertime is a time of great renewal. It is the time of year when nature's smooth blanket of white may emphasize purity and innocence, even cleansing. It is a time of comfort and of blessing. It is the time of year when God Himself takes care to protect and preserve all the sleeping, dormant life until the

135

spring.

* * * * *

Susan spent what she had of the money on heating oil and food. The rest went into Marvin's front pocket.

* * * * *

December almost forces us to stop, to take our deepest breaths and to sit down. To sit down and remember how it is that we have arrived at this station in life.

* * * * *

I thanked God that year that Susan did not have any children. It was difficult enough to watch her suffer through what she was suffering with only the Lord to help her. As I watched my nieces and my nephew playing with their toys on Christmas morning, I wondered how she would have fared. Would a child have made things better or worse under those circumstances?

* * * * *

Winter teaches us that there is a lot of peace found simply in letting everything go. Watch the little children as they allow themselves to fall trustfully backward, completing their happiness by falling, by turning themselves into feathery angels in the snow.

* * * * *

Our church held a midnight service on New Year's Eve that year. I attended, but later finished my night out at the tavern.

Susan had been there, but she did not smile very much from what I had seen. At eleven thirty, she confided in me that her husband had not been home for three long days.

* * * * *

Winter's berries,
turned to wine,
their ruby colors tainting time.
Drink from the cup
of winter's sweet sounds,
for the living,
the dead,
the lost,
and the found.

* * * * *

It is not easy being a man trying to remain a Christian in a sin-filled world. Stories such as Susan's still retained the ability to draw from within me the anger I had so dutifully tried to suppress. I do not know what it is like to be a practicing, saved Christian woman, but in seeing the sullen depressions that were Susan's eyes late that evening, I know it must sometimes be rough.

Sometime after midnight, Susan asked me where I was going. I told her, "Out to the tavern," the only place that served liquor and beer in our town. She told me she wanted to join me and I asked her if she thought that would be smart, or even appropriate. She told me, "No," but that anything would be better than another lonely night at home waiting for Marvin to return.

I told her she would have to meet me there if she wanted to join me.

She did.

* * * * *

Winter hides our naked bodies within layers of warm clothing, putting our faces on more prominent and honest display.

* * * * *

I ordered a glass of whiskey with a beer chaser. Susan ordered coffee. Later she said she was surprised to see me consume so much drink.

We talked about many things that evening until the bar closed. When she asked if there was somewhere we could go in order to continue with the conversation, I told her, "No," but that if she were to go home and get some rest, we could speak in the morning over coffee at the church.

The New Year's party had been entertaining, but Susan was afraid to go home to face the prospect of the darkness all alone. It was sad that I could not help her.

* * * * *

Somewhere in the breast of winter beats a heart restfully awaiting tomorrow's rebirth.

* * * * *

She told me she thought she might actually die from despair if Marvin chose once again not to come home.

"Hap-py New Year!"

"It has been three nights in a row, John. If he doesn't come home tonight, he'd better be dead."

Marvin was already home by the time Susan got home and his excuse was that he ran into some of the boys, had gotten carried away, and had forgotten to call her.

Susan chose to believe him.

"Hap-py New Year!"

* * * * *

December 31st is like a snake with pale blue eyes, with the midnight coming on tenuously as the burly one peels off his skin. It leaves us all freshly renewed on that first of many

January mornings, awkwardly awakening, like new children, born of the old, anxious for our new lives to begin.

*   *   *   *   *

1974.

I was soon to turn thirty, and I was still single, but I still felt so young. Susan did not feel so young, nor did she come by for that early morning cup of coffee at the church. In fact, I did not hear from her for many days to come.

Rarely were there many single women in our congregation. As I recall, there were not very many even close to my age. Teenage girls and widows, everyone else was either married or allergic to the altar.

1974 was not a very big year for church populations. Something about the seventies seemed to be drawing much of the younger generation away from faith and into sin. Maybe it was the war, maybe it was the politics, or maybe it was the music and all of the drugs. Maybe it was the freedom. Maybe it was change. There was that steadily growing divorce rate… temptation all around. It could have had a lot to do with Nietzsche's "God is dead" proclamation and Time Magazine's infamous cover, "Is God Dead?" which challenged a lot of society to rethink their alliances. There was also all that 'free sex' which some had confused with free love, or maybe it was just the socio-spiritual tide going out once again. I still do not know to this day. All I know is that Marvin had a woman who loved him with all that God had given her and that was not enough for him. She loved him deeply and faithfully, and yet I was still alone.

Life is beautiful, say some.

*   *   *   *   *

Winter does not discriminate. It will steal the breath from the warm and the cold; milk the life from the innocent, the guilty, and the free. It will lay bare and blue the beautiful, and the untrue, lay to rest both the young and the old, both the same.

* * * * *

God blessed Susan's family in mid January when Marvin landed a job in the warehouse an automobile manufacturer had built just out of town. His experiences in the army afforded him the opportunity, as he possessed the training requirements and skills to operate all of their mobile machinery. He became an operator, earning nearly twice as much as I was earning as sexton of the church. Susan was able to give back the car she had borrowed from her cousin, as Marvin had chosen to buy her a used one. They even invested in some new furniture. He did not give up his romance with Teesha Daniels, but at least in some ways he was being a man.

Susan's health began improving. She was eating again. She looked fit. On Sundays, she even seemed a little more cheerful, yet she never did manage to lose those dark circles which had appeared sadly back in November, one under each of her eyes.

* * * * *

Winter drifts and billows, stirring us to dress and to carry in the wood. Nothing gets us moving, up, and off the bed and into our heaviest of boots, like the sight of a slowly dying fire in the cold.

* * * * *

Susan had not prayed in church for two weeks, other than on Sundays, and when asked she would simply explain that all her prayers had been answered, and how abundantly she had been blessed.

"You think that because he bought you a car and a dinette and a new couch that he's changed?"

Mid-sentence, that day, was the first time I realized, really accepted, that my love for her was beyond inappropriate.

There was only one option. I had to walk away from her and I had to do it fast.

Nevertheless, nothing worked. The more I tried to avoid her, the more she sought me out. She began showing up at the church after work just to share stories with me about the children at school. She would tell me the funny stories, the sad ones, and the ones that made her smile. I would come up with many excuses to get away from her, but she would only follow after.

I would pray to God for her to let me be. I would pray for Marvin to run away with his girlfriend. I would pray for every possible scenario that might bring us together or separate us forever until I had to accept that it was entirely my fault to begin with.

The problem was not that I had fallen in love with another man's wife; the problem was that I was incapable of loving a woman without wanting her all to myself.

I needed correction.

As a Christian man, I needed to become a man who had the capacity for real love, not just the kind of love that gets a man something in return.

At the time, and I now know this; I was incapable of being Susan's friend.

* * * * *

Darkness is the skater abruptly swallowed by the ice.

* * * * *

In February, I got down on my knees and prayed for God to help me solve my dilemma. I prayed to the Father, asking Him to open my heart and to show me the way.

"Father, you have brought the most beautiful, lost..." and that is when I realized what was really truly going on with me.

"Lost..."

There it was in front of me.

"Lost."

I did not "Love" Susan in the conventional sense of the word; I was infatuated with her, and I wanted to save her from her distress. I was trying to rescue again…

I could damn the truth to Hell sometimes.

*   *   *   *   *

Winter can often feel timeless, timeless and unchanging, uncommonly known as the calm before the spring.

*   *   *   *   *

I dutifully set to trying to understand if there was any way in which I could truly help Susan as a friend, without falling into the trap of becoming the white knight, and without wanting anything more. I took account of my past actions: When all she needed from me was an ear to listen, I had always offered her advice. It was time to stop that practice. I needed correction.

When all she needed was a friend to hold her, I turned away, sighting Ecclesiastes 3:5 in my defense: *A time for embracing, and a time to refrain from embracing.*

When she was broke, I gave her money. Some say two out of three ain't so bad.

However, when she needed me to love her, I wanted her all to my own, and that is where I had it all wrong, to say the very least.

*   *   *   *   *

Winter wants to tell us all a story.

*   *   *   *   *

I did the only thing I thought I could do as a man. I pulled my boots up and paid a visit to Marvin.

The day I chose to do this was a Friday: March 3, 1974, and I will always remember that date because I still have a scar on my face to remind me of what I had done.

I knew where Marvin would take Teesha when they wanted to meet up for cocktails. I knew because he had told me about the place back in the fall.

I thought, well, if Marvin was a creature of habit, then he would be meeting up with her after his shift. Right I was.

It was payday. Marvin had a wad of fresh bills in his pocket and Teesha was wearing a coat he had bought just for her. I sat watching from my truck as they got out of his car and walked in through the door together.

The little bar was about twelve miles from the edge of town in the next town over. It was a dark, little blue-collar place where misery loved company and all walks of life got along.

It was not a very Christian establishment.

It was the kind of place where men such as Marvin went when they did not wish to be recognized or exposed for what they were doing. People there did not make introductions, and when they did, they used nicknames and slang. Last names were unheard of.

Marvin and Teesha sat in a booth together. I saw them when I entered. He was casually kissing her hand.

* * * * *

Winter leaves a slippery trap for those who feel that looking down is beneath them.

* * * * *

March is a strange month. By March, most people have gotten tired of the cold. They long for the easiness of spring, and as I learned that day, it is a very bad month to stand between a young woman and her sugar daddy.

I only knew Teesha Daniels' name because I had met her once when I was just a boy. Teesha grew up in my hometown, which was smaller, and a poorer town. We were the exception because my family owned a farm.

Teesha Daniels developed quite early for her age, and all of

143

us boys were drawn to her, despite the rampant prejudice in our township, and we would take any opportunity to check her out.

Back when I was twelve, Teesha would lift up her shirt for a quarter.

* * * * *

Springtime inherits all that winter leaves behind.

* * * * *

I walked in and ordered a round of drinks for their table. Then I waited for Marvin to invite me to sit down. He did not.

Instead, he came over to the bar to greet me, and when he did, I think he already knew what I had gone there to say.

"So, what brings you around these parts, Johnny Boy?"

He had his own pack of smokes. That much I noticed right away.

"I thought it would be a good idea if we had a little talk." I said this quite seriously.

"Oh," and finally, there was that smile, "I see... let me guess." He laughed, looked back at Teesha, and then he looked me up and down once, "You're still sweet on my wife. Is that what this is about?"

It would not have hurt more if he had just gone and kicked me in the groin.

"John, John, John..." he put his hand on my shoulder, "When are you going to learn that Susan is never going to leave me? Give it up, Brother; she and I are doing just fine, just like it's supposed to be. You see that car she's driving? She's happy. Leave it alone." Then he took his hand off my shoulder, "C'mon, let's have a drink. Come sit down."

I was not there to be friendly. Fact was I no longer knew why I was there.

As we walked to the table and then sat down, I did my best to recall my purpose. I had thought my mission was to try to convince Marvin to give up his adulterous activities, to repent,

144

and to be a good man. Perhaps I was there to plant the seed. Nevertheless, there I was: guilty as charged. He could see right through me.

"Marvin…"

He was laughing at me, "O.K.," and Teesha seemed to be laughing also, "If it makes you feel any better go ahead and say your piece."

The two of them thought it was funny.

I wanted to explain to him that Jesus wants us to live good lives, and that his actions were destroying the most wonderful soul I had ever encountered, and how each of their lives, even Teesha Daniel's, would improve if he would just accept that he was a married man and discontinue with his treacherous sin. But I did not.

In place of those words, I said, "Marvin, you're killing Susan. Every single day you take a little bit more of her… you're taking away from her spirit and she is way too beautiful a person to deserve that."

Marvin did not flinch, he just said, "Brother, the Lord made women to please us," and he pulled Teesha closer to him, "look around you… why don't you go and find yourself one of your own and let this thing go before it drives you crazy, or worse, before we end up in a disagreement or something." Then he leaned in to kiss Teesha Daniels on the cheek, "Just stay away from what is mine, O.K.? Mine are already taken."

The soft, brown skin of Teesha's face shown in the dim bar lighting. She was very attractive. Her skin tone appeared to darken as she lowered her eyes in a simple display of what appeared to be shame or coy amusement, looking down at the table.

"Now come on Brother," and Marvin was smiling again, "Have a drink with us and relax. Maybe one of Teesha's friends will join us for a beer. She could introduce you to someone real nice, take it from me. What do you say?" He was holding up his beer bottle as if to toast.

"I can't do that Marvin. If I join you, I am afraid I might ruin your evening."

Marvin seemed too confident for his own good, "I doubt

you'd ruin my evening and Teesha don't give a rat's ass about Susan, so you can talk all you want. Hell, she'd be as happy as you if Susan and I was to split up, but that's just not going to happen."

I remained seated at the table, and after completing what I had gone there to say, Teesha added, "I keep telling him to leave her. He don't belong with no white woman anyhow. I think he just stays with her to make you and I mad." She was laughing about it while rubbing Marvin's leg.

I finished my drink and they thanked me for the round and bid me a cheerful farewell. I walked out so angry I was cursing under my breath and before I could make it to the door of my truck, I slipped on a puddle of ice and landed face first on the bitter, frozen ground.

My nose required three stitches.

* * * * *

The last snowfall of winter is often the coldest of all.

* * * * *

That is how it all went, on and off, for the next several months of our lives. It was Marvin and Teesha, Marvin and Susan, with me often dating, but never once finding anyone who could compare to the soul I discovered that August 28th within that pretty girl.

It was evil.

It was insanity.

And it was sin.

However, I never once broke my promise to God, even when Susan tried to kiss me that following spring.

* * * * *

They say March comes in like a lion and out like a lamb. Next, they say that April showers bring May flowers. What they forget to tell you is that Hell hath no greater temptress than a woman at the end of her string.

* * * * *

There was barely one cord of wood remaining when winter finally loosed its grasp and gave up its hold to sweet sister spring. Everyone was tired of winter. I was mostly tired of the cold.

A month after Marvin and I had our little talk at the bar, Teesha announced that she was pregnant. What Marvin would never know, and what Teesha Daniels would never tell him, was that the baby was not his.

When Teesha Daniels showed up at Marvin and Susan's front door to share the good news with them, Susan came quite close to passing out.

From whence does the eternal spring of inspiration flow? It flows like a nosebleed straight from the nose. It is like cathartic menstruation, and it flows like a violent, unsounded scream. Spring never warns us that it is coming, it merely seduces us with warmer rays, tiny flower blossoms, angelic skies filled with little yellow and golden-green leaf buds. Then, once seduced, it punches us right in the face.

* * * * *

Hours later, after receiving the news concerning Teesha Daniels' pregnancy, Susan drove her car into a fence, backed up over her garbage cans, and then headed in my direction to seek out her savior, and me, at the church. Unfortunately, she bought a bottle of wine on the way and found me first.

That was quite possibly the most difficult day of my life.

* * * * *

Spring is a bitch in heat.

* * * * *

"The church is locked."

I looked back toward the church quizzically, "No it's not. It's never locked."

She was sitting in the cemetery when I found her. Susan was sitting in the grass with her back against the old fieldstone wall beneath one of the trees. There was an open bottle of wine in her lap. The neck of the bottle was clear down to far below where the glass of the bottle widened, so I could see that she had already consumed a good portion of the wine. There was a cork floating upon the surface of the dark red liquid inside.

"I didn't have a corkscrew," and she was laughing unsteadily, "So I pushed the cork in with a stick." She was looking at the bottle in her hand, "I never knew that worked, but it does." Susan took a long, slow gulp from her wine. The bottle was soon half-empty.

The wine in the bottle was dark beneath the green glass; so red that it looked to me as if Susan had been nursing a very large vile of blood.

"Are you alright?" I asked her.

From where I was standing, I could see most of Susan's underwear due to her legs-up position in the grass against the wall along with the risen up skirt she was wearing. Most of me did not want to see that. I stepped to the side after taking one last sinful peek. She noticed and she smiled.

"Can I have a cigarette?" She asked looking up at me, smiling further, knowing damn well I got a good glimpse of her yellowy cotton. It was all on purpose; all for her benefit, and for mine.

"Sure," so I rolled her one.

I rolled her that cigarette a little too quickly though, and it came out a little pregnant in the middle, so I stuck that one behind my ear and proceeded to roll her another. Less hastily, this one came out all right, nearly perfect as cigarettes go. I had no idea what was troubling her. I was doing my best to erase the thought of what I had seen... that triangular patch of soft yellow between her forbidden legs.

After lighting her smoke and handing it to her, I sat down

148

next to her by the wall. Then I asked her what was wrong. She could not speak the words at first, and that is how I guessed them.

*   *   *   *   *

Springtime is not all fuzzy baby bunnies and little yellow goslings following their mothers down the road. It is not all butterflies and pansies. It is a time of violent aggression, a time for territoriality. When members of the same sex within the same species will kill one another with tooth, antler, and claw for food and the prospect of mating. Spring is a time of wanton animalistic pheromone induced brazen outdoor sexuality. Yet, it can also be a season of great hope and inspiration, even a time for the most delicate of loves.

*   *   *   *   *

"I just found out they are…"
Susan was breaking.
"They just…"
I knew precisely what Susan was about to say. I guess in a way I had foreseen this day's arrival all along.

She took another long, deep pull from the bottle. It was not a good thing. Susan was unaccustomed to drinking more than a single glass. I thought for sure that at any moment she would be sick.

"I can't have babies, John." The tears and the snot began to flow.

Susan was really breaking down. Her sobs echoed in such stark contrast to that lovely April day. I could hear them echo back as they met with the stillness of the pond.

There were daffodils blooming all around us. Some were in sunlight, others in the shade. Small clusters of jonquils, and taller daffodils; bulbs left behind by people who cared for the dead. In the unkempt grass of the graveyard, they looked as if they had been blooming for eons, spread around here and there, tucked away besides the gravestones and in the corner

149

by the gate in that old stone wall.

Susan was shaking, but then she suddenly went still.

* * * * *

Springtime is a snapping turtle lurking beneath the darkest edge of the most inviting pool of water.

* * * * *

"God won't let me have any children, and yet He is going to let the two of them bring one into the world..." She was looking down at the bottle that now rested between her two bare feet.

I did not know what to say then.

When I turned my head to look at her, she was staring ahead like a villain plotting her crime.

* * * * *

A little bit of winter always remains within the spring.

* * * * *

If only Susan had known it was not her fault. If only she had gone to a doctor.

* * * * *

Springtime cannot tell you its troubles; it will only show you the good.

* * * * *

Back in the fall, I had noticed that many caterpillars do not become butterflies or moths until the following spring. They winter over on the farm in their cocoons. That was a surprise to me. I had always imagined it happened all at once. What

150

surprised me most was how these thin, little naked creatures, so defenseless and so small, could curl up into little wombs, a dead leaf, some spun silk, some musical, magical miniscule bands of wind and sunshine, and successfully weather the cold.

Susan began to cocoon then right before my eyes.

*   *   *   *   *

Winter touches springtime through the fingers of her swiftly flowing waters, kissing her roots and blossoms with gifts of satisfaction, breezes born of mountaintops, the trickling waters from the hillsides marching; matching the sleepy cadence of the thaw within the ground.

*   *   *   *   *

Susan not only went mad that morning, smashing her empty bottle of wine upon one of the oldest of headstones, but she kicked and she screamed and then she fell to the ground. She shouted at God through the cloudscape like a disgruntled volunteer soldier, even demanding that He come right down and set things straight.

As we sat there afterwards, me, a little spooked by her actions, and she a little muddied, all we heard otherwise was the trickle of birdsong flowing through the trees.

*   *   *   *   *

Sometimes your spring is in the eyes of another. Sometimes your fall is in the eyes of the same.

*   *   *   *   *

If you look closely enough, spring can remind each one of us that no matter how deeply planted into the muck of this life, within each of us, we are blessed with the ever-present ability to rise up slowly, to grow through it, and to bring forth

151

amicably each of our fruits.

I have seen plenty of people, but most often women, cry directly in front of me without fear of embarrassment or reproach. My mother's tears were always the toughest and most heart wrenching to endure. However, never once before that day in the cemetery, alone with poor Susan, had I ever witnessed a woman scream like that before. It was like watching someone being murdered from inside.

*   *   *   *   *

Spring is a trickster, a prankster, a thief. Spring is the insect that looks like a leaf. Springtime's mirage will beckon you to swim, but dare you, oh dare you, ever go in?

*   *   *   *   *

It was as if she were a mother swan having just watched a snapping turtle devour the last of her babies.

Susan was screaming for the hopeless zero that burned within her heart, dying over and over again inside for all her many sons and daughters that would never, ever be. And there was nothing I could do to fix it.

I was nothing more than the sexton of a church, the repairman. Not a pastor. Not God. I was a man barely capable of being a true friend.

*   *   *   *   *

Spring sends us racing, blindly and madly, basically into nowhere at all.

*   *   *   *   *

Personally, I believe God had given Susan her back door out the day she discovered Marvin's infidelity. I believe this because it came right out of our Savior's mouth, *"Let no man turn asunder that which God has brought together in His*

152

name. Lest for the cause of adultery, let no persons divorce."

And now there was a baby on the way.

Susan had been given every opportunity to be free. Most of all, she even had me there waiting. However, Susan believed in something; she believed in the preeminence and the permanence of forgiveness. Either that or she was scared of something else even more.

There sat I, like some jealous, lustful, forsaken little troll in the graveyard, and I watched as the woman I loved shouted helplessly up to the sky. Worst of all was the fact that I could not even hold her, let alone get the thought of her yellow panties out of my mind.

$$* \quad * \quad * \quad * \quad *$$

Springtime is lust, and lust is a shining, glittering fishing lure covered in terrible hooks.

$$* \quad * \quad * \quad * \quad *$$

Susan, surprisingly enough, was able to hold her booze for most of that day. She did not get sick, but what she did do was to grab my face and try to kiss me right there in the graveyard. No one would have ever seen us, hidden as we were by the stones in that old graveyard wall, but I had to pull away just the same.

I did not mean it that way, but my rejection of her, for the second time, was like a rusted nail in the coffin of her elusive deliverance. So I made her a deal: I told her that if she left her husband, and married me, I would kiss her on our wedding day.

She laughed at me and told me to, "Grow a pair of balls, John" and that is when I knew it was definitely the wine.

Then she spit in my face and I knew it could only be Satan; either Satan or the pain of a woman near her end.

$$* \quad * \quad * \quad * \quad *$$

Spring is when life just seems to appear out of nowhere, for no reason whatsoever at all.

* * * * *

Eventually Susan walked off and passed out while lying down in a sunnier patch in the field. I did not bother to wake her. I simply sat and watched her while she slept it off amongst the flowers and the raiment of the lesser creatures of this world.

* * * * *

The Earth is a nearly round world. Perfectly spherical, it is not, but what goes around in autumn surely comes around in spring.

* * * * *

Susan had spent the entire winter cocooned within her misery, hoping and praying that her life would miraculously change. To her dismay, and to the increase of her despair, she had made two dire mistakes. The first was the same mistake many people make whenever they pray.

Susan failed to recognize the necessity of being specific with her prayers.

The second mistake she made was to not recognize and utilize the many gifts God had already blessed her with to aid her in her plight, and in her confusion, she mistook giving in and giving up with giving her will over to the Lord. In giving in, she failed to allow God to help her solve her own problems. In giving up, she failed herself and forsook the gift.

You cannot just throw up your hands and turn your will over to God without remembering free will. God will never take free will from you. You also need to follow the guidance, the instructions, and the ever-present signs and wonders, which always abound.

Susan was finding all this out the hard way.

*   *   *   *   *

I sat in the grass like a good friend or like any passive sucker in my position might and I prayed over Susan for nearly two hours until she awoke. When Susan was finally upright and talking coherently, she could hardly recall any of what had transpired. All she knew, she said, was that she had some vague recollection of drinking wine in the cemetery and then shouting at me for some reason and calling me names.

I let her have that back door out and let it all go at that. Secretly, I was regretting the fact that I had made the right choice though.

I could still taste the wine from her lips.

*   *   *   *   *

Spring is a chartreuse explosion of light. Spring is a chartreuse explosion of life.

*   *   *   *   *

Marvin and Teesha were going to have a child. Neither discussed the subject much, and once again, their actions were taking a toll upon Susan's health and her body. Once again, Susan was steadily growing thinner. Her eyes looked dark and she never looked very happy anymore.

Susan was smoking two packs a day by the end of May. She had also taken up drinking.

*   *   *   *   *

We shed our heavy clothing in the springtime, trading them in for much softer wares. We begin to relax once again, enjoying the changes in the weather as the gentler season rolls in. We feel our blessings in spring, but mostly because we have made it to the other side of winter unscathed.

*   *   *   *   *

155

Susan was not feeling very blessed at all. Marvin was spending more time away from home, and Susan had stopped attending church. Pastor and his wife even tried to speak with her.

"God's word is in the words of the book Susan, your answers are in there, and as you read, you must listen as He speaks His word directly into your heart."

They tried their best to get through to her.

"It is a living word, and the word changes with you, to meet your changing needs at each step along the way. If only you would return to the word and try to see that God will speak to you concerning your troubles."

I tried, but even I could not get through.

* * * * *

Springtime favors the happily coupled.

* * * * *

With spring came spring cleaning, the mowing, the weeding, repairs to the rooftop and screens. As sexton of the church, my responsibility was to clean the bats out of the attic, the wasp nests and leaves from the gutters, and to make sure no rainwater would ever get through to those places it did not belong. It was my job to fix broken things…

When I first met Susan, she was my ideal of the perfect young woman. However, what I learned was that Susan was living in a dream. She was perfect for me, and circumstance did not change this, but now, nine months to the day we had met, Susan was a much older woman; living more so in a current nightmare than her dream of long ago.

If only she had been willing to listen to what I think God was saying all along.

* * * * *

Springtime is a clutch of crocus singing in the snow. You

156

can forgive the ones that hurt you, but you can also let them go…

*   *   *   *   *

That year, Bob Dylan sang out the soundtrack to our lives, but I do not think he knew he was doing it specifically for us. At least I had someone else to relate to besides Jesus, John, Paul, George and Ringo.

By the end of May, Susan had begun to have nosebleeds. The doctors told her it was anemia, and they suggested that she try to put on a little weight. I only wish they had taken the time to do more tests.

May. May is April plus one, and in other words; Teesha's child would enter the world to greet his family and father come December.

Susan would not live to see that day. I think God may have blessed her with that, come to think of it now. Yet, even still, I think it could have all gone differently if she had only believed.

Susan began taking iron pills on May 5th and she came by to visit me at the church the day she bought her prescription. She was thin and extremely pale, and her chest bones and collar were showing about the neckline of her shirt. Susan was visibly shaking as we stood outside the doors to the church puffing on two of her Camels. She told me unhappily that it was the third pack she had opened that day.

Marvin was still out of town.

*   *   *   *   *

Spring is the usher delivering us all to summer's seating, reserved. Spring is like a matron, someone who knows what has been, and often times what is to come. Spring is a monster; energy released in every direction, all at once. Spring is a feather falling gently from the sky.

Springtime is mud in your eye.

*   *   *   *   *

We talked about Jesus' words and what he taught. We talked about how much we need to learn to forgive ourselves as well as learning to forgive others. Then we laughed as we realized that no one could truly forgive us for our sins, except for God. And how afterwards it is often necessary to forgive one's self.

We talked about suffering, and although Susan did not convince me, it seemed as though she had come to compare her suffering within her marriage to the sufferings of Paul.

*   *   *   *   *

Spring is the capital of the states of indecision and confusion.

*   *   *   *   *

"God does not want you to suffer."

"That's not what my Bible says."

"Susan, the Bible says that suffering is good for us. It says that we should rejoice through our suffering. It even says that we should feel blessed for both suffering and for good, but nowhere does it say that we should choose suffering or seek suffering or that God ever wants for us to suffer."

She took a pull from her cigarette and asked, "Then what is the point?"

I told her I had to get back to work then. I had to get back on the roof.

*   *   *   *   *

Spring is a lacey, white veil that hides a hideous volume. Spring is a mask. Spring holds all the answers to the questions we are too afraid to ask.

*   *   *   *   *

158

Susan died of lung cancer on the first day of winter, December 21st, 1974. They had diagnosed her with anemia, but they were wrong.

Marvin did not even show up to her funeral.

Despite my anger, I forgave him… for his sake and for mine.

*   *   *   *   *

Spring is like an angel guiding us and protecting us through our childhood, but as soon as summer comes, she lets us go…

*   *   *   *   *

June.

July.

I spent many of my afternoons fishing that year. The bass in the pond out back of the church were plentiful, and during summer, well, I ate my fair share of skillet-fried bass and potatoes. Susan would often stop down to go swimming. I would not swim with her because she liked to swim in the nude, and I think she would do it to tempt me because, otherwise, that was definitely not her style.

Time and time again that spring and early summer I would repeat to her the deal I had presented to her the day she smashed her bottle on the grave. *Divorce him, and I will marry you!* However, mostly I just mumbled it under my breath as I was walking away from the pond with my pole, listening to the sounds of her splashing around naked in the sun.

*   *   *   *   *

Summer is a Godsend, but then again, all the seasons are, and the seasons of and the reasons for our lives are ever changing.

*   *   *   *   *

As I had said before, my feelings are that Susan went a little mad the day she discovered her husband was having a baby with another woman. The fact was though, that he was not. Marvin could not impregnate a woman. He was impotent. However, Susan would not know this until after she was gone.

*   *   *   *   *

How do seeds survive the winter, once planted in your soul?

*   *   *   *   *

Susan's madness manifested itself in an expression of seduction, but not of her choosing, for she was physiologically losing her mind. Unbeknownst to any of us, her cancer had already metastasized, and it was slowly affecting her brain. Apparently, this physiological change within her began with the shock of Teesha's news regarding her pregnancy. The news traumatized Susan's system, and it cut her defenses down.

She weighed approximately 78 pounds when the flowers of June were just blooming, and although her eyes were bright, her mind was beginning to go. No one knew this, not even Susan.

In many ways, Susan may have wanted to feel that she was still attractive, who can say. Often, she would just show up next to me while I was fishing and she would smile and begin to undress without saying a word. Sometimes, she would even try to talk to me while she was topless; arriving at my side without a shirt. However, I would not sin with her in that manner, nor would I allow myself to add to everyone's grief by falling prey to her temptation.

She was sick, and no one really knew the extent of her unseen illness, and perhaps she wanted some revenge, yet I was standing my ground.

Leave it to a woman to figure out a way to spoil a fine day of fishing.

* * * * *

Spring is thunder. Spring is the rain that melts the snow. At the end of winter, and the end of summer, we feel the winds of change begin to blow.

* * * * *

I am convinced to this day that Susan would not have developed cancer had it not been for all the social pressure, magnified and compounded by her husband Marvin's sin. In 1974, she was only 26 years old. She had been healthy most of her life. She was beautiful, and she was doing her best to live right.

I have never blamed the Lord for taking her away from me, for taking her from us. If anything, I blame her confusion and her stubbornness, but most of all I will always blame Marvin Watts for her death.

I do not hate him. I have forgiven him. Nevertheless, I put the blame where the blame belongs.

* * * * *

Summer is like flying with your eyes closed.

* * * * *

Susan was a spirit unlike any I had ever come to know. She was ruthlessly engaging and altogether beauteous to the core.

The spring of 1974 was difficult, even heartbreaking for me, but I had to learn how to deal with Susan as someone I could love in true platonic fashion. That was all. If you knew all that God had done for me, you would understand.

Susan still looked terribly downtrodden and physically drained, so I thought I would start inviting her to join me in less tempting activities, outdoors.

"I'll make a deal with you. Whenever Marvin goes missing, just come and find me and we can go for a hike."

Susan agreed.

Why was I doing it? I still do not know. All I know is that God brought her into my life and I honestly loved her, or at least I felt something very strong for her in my heart.

The infatuation was still there, but I was diverting it, or perhaps I was simply walking a very thin line. I won't deny it. I loved having Susan around even under such abhorrent conditions. She was like a source of energy for me, unparalleled by any other source of inspiration I have ever known.

I still have all of her poetry…

* * * * *

Spring is the garden
of every summer's delight.
Whereas springtime coasts
upon time's flow,
autumn will put up a fight.

* * * * *

We would walk along the forest paths whenever Marvin would be out wandering, enjoying our long conversations and everything nature had to offer. Almost everything, that is.

By the time July arrived, we were spending over 30 hours a week together. Quite often, it took all the energy I had just to get her to smile. Then one day, one sunny July afternoon, just when I thought I had everything under control, I snapped and I confronted her.

The trees were all moving, waving their branches, carelessly generating a wonderful breeze, when I finally decided to speak up, "Susan, I have to know something."

She stopped mid stride on the path.

"Why won't you leave him?"

I was breaking my promise to God.

"Do you not see how happy we could be together? How… how made for each other we are?"

162

There was no use in stopping, so I just kept right on going.

"Ever since the day we first met, I have wanted nothing more than to be with you... and we are perfect together, and you are miserable with him! What in the world could make you want to stay with that man when you would be justified in leaving him? When I am standing right here?"

I knew it was a sin to tempt her, but I said it all anyway.

Susan was standing perfectly still I remember, looking contemplative and secure. Then she said a group of words that nearly tore me apart.

"Because I do not believe in it, John. All I have ever known is suffering and that is what I have now. And this 'made for each other' perfection crap? You say we are perfect? Well, all I see is something incredible. I see an illusion, a mirage. What I see is a person with whom I have a tremendous amount in common, and a very deep connection. You are like no one else I have ever met before. You are like the male version of me and that is crazy... I wouldn't even know where to begin or what to do with that! I think I would go insane just waiting for the day that the other shoe would drop. Can't you see that?"

I was stupefied. All I could muster was a great, big, "What?"

"See? You don't get that, and that is the biggest, and maybe the only difference between you and me. John..." and she began moving around, I remember that, "my mother died when I was eleven years old and I had to spend the next seven years in foster care moving from house to house, from one set of nut-jobs or perverts to the next. I was a ward of the state and life sucked, John. It really, really sucked for me. After graduation, I even tried to go to college, but I had no foundation and I failed. I became a prostitute at twenty years old. A prostitute! I was a drug addict by twenty-one, and then Marvin came along and rescued me and this is all I have and this is where I am now."

She was breathing so hard that her shallow chest looked like an accordion.

"I am saved and now I have a foundation and that means everything to me. Maybe it is not the best, but I have a home, and a car, and I do regular things. I have my job working with

163

children!" Her shout echoed aimlessly through the wood. "Children, John! Do you know what that means to me?"

I could not believe my ears. My legs were shaking.

She whispered coarsely, "And when I die... I am going to Heaven, John, and no one, no one is ever going to take that away from me now." She said this so softly, and so slowly, it was as if she was crying each one of those words.

Susan was looking at me as if I hadn't a clue, when suddenly I realized I had not.

Susan already had everything she would ever need.

* * * * *

Summer is the balancing of breath as we recognize the air for all it truly is.

* * * * *

I never knew any of those things about Susan. I had always assumed she just liked black men, and hence, her gravitation towards Marvin Watts. Things had begun to make a little more sense. Not that there was anything wrong with the fact that she had fallen in love with him, it just seemed to me at the time we had met that theirs was a very odd pairing.

"What you see, John, is the potential for a wonderful friendship, but you won't look away from the fact that I am a woman long enough to just love me like a friend and let it be. Yes, I like you, John. And yes, I even love you John, but I also love my husband for everything he ever did for me and maybe it is because you have never fully given yourself to anyone that you cannot relate to that."

She was burning.

"John, I have room enough and love enough in my heart to love more than just one man, and I can do that without wanting anything more from any other man but my husband. It is you that has the problem, and I know that you won't hug me or hold me when I need you to because it is you that is afraid that you will not want to let go."

164

I could not tell whether she was dead on, or dead wrong. The fact was, I did not trust either one of us, and I thought that was being fair. Apparently, I was mistaken.

"You are blaming me, calling me a woman who is subject to temptation during a rough patch in my marriage when it is really you that is afraid of letting go."

I could not believe what she was saying.

"I'll prove it! Here…" and she held out her hand, "Hold my hand and walk with me. Here, c'mon…" and she was looking directly into my eyes. "We are way out here in the woods and no one is going to see us, John. We can walk and we can talk and we can feel close to each other and not even God would say that was wrong."

My head was spinning. I could feel all Marvin's words falling like rain, his laughter falling like pellets of hail down upon me. I felt the weight of her crystalline eyes staring through me, the weight of the truth, and I hated myself then.

Nevertheless, this was another man's wife, and everything inside of me told me that she would never tell him that we had held hands, so therefore, it was inappropriate behavior.

Susan was still thrusting out her hand in my direction.

"What's the matter, John, are you afraid of me? You want me to divorce my husband so I can marry you, and you won't even hold my hand in friendship?"

None of it was fair. None of it at all.

"You are afraid of me, aren't you? I knew it! You want this 'perfection' John, but what I am is real… and that is what I am afraid of."

"What?" I said quickly because I had gotten lost in everything she was saying, "Explain that to me."

"John, the moment you figure out that I am a real, living, breathing, imperfect human being you would be done with me. I can see it all now. Slowly but surely, you'd start to pick me apart until there was nothing really left of me at all. That's not perfection, John. That sounds a lot to me like Hell."

In my mind, I was wondering if what she was saying was really the truth, or if it was only her way of convincing herself that nothing in her life would ever be good, or satisfying, or

165

anything close to healthy at all.

To this day, I still do not know.

*   *   *   *   *

Summer is like asking your parents if you can stay up just one hour longer. Then it is like hitting the snooze button on the mechanism that makes us all grow old.

*   *   *   *   *

I didn't like what I was hearing. Susan was pigeon holing me into the category of being a teenager living in a romantic fantasy world. She was acting as if I was some immature day dreamer, some guy who could not even decipher what he wanted from life and whom he got along with.

Mine was not a fantasy of perfection, and my interest in her went far beyond mere physical attraction. I never thought she was perfect, I just thought she was perfect for me.

Susan was a person I wanted to spend my every moment with, and for her, it had always appeared that I was that person too.

I thought '*What about last year? How about all those times she wanted to be around me? What woman or man would not want to spend their life with the person they most want to spend their time with?* It was all so simple a formula for me. At the time, I could not believe that Susan could not see that.

I could no longer understand what was going on.

Susan continued to berate and attack me. We stood there on the path in the forest, engulfed in a conflagration of spirit somewhere between Heaven and Hell that day.

*   *   *   *   *

Summertime stretches so far into the evening; it is a wonder how we ever get to sleep.

*   *   *   *   *

166

When she finally stopped yelling at me, I gave her a little piece of my mind.

"You know, Susan; you are so lost in your own need to prove to yourself that life is nothing more than something to loathe and detest and merely survive that the only way you can enjoy anything even close to interesting or compelling is if you can keep it over here to the side. You are passionate, probably the most passionate woman I have ever loved, but you cast your pearls before swine because you are petrified that someone you actually love might honestly love you back and accept you. Maybe it is because you lost your mom that you are afraid to really love someone, someone you might actually lose someday, but you cannot avoid that in life, Susan, and doing so is killing you! You are going to love no matter who you are with, and in the end that makes you vulnerable, and that is why you look and feel as if you are dying. You are afraid to love, and so you have laid yourself on the chopping block for a man that does not deserve you so he can destroy every ounce of what you are and that's a sin!"

In one manner of speaking; that was the closest I ever got to holding Susan's hand. When I was finished shouting, Susan hauled off and slapped me right across my face.

* * * * *

Summer can be a time of great celebration, or it can be a time to be repulsed by the very pores within your skin. It can be hot and muggy, murderous, uneasy to endure, humid, yet it can also be the most enjoyable time of the year.

* * * * *

"You are seriously suffering from a case of misplaced affection." She said these words so sternly it was as if I was a little boy in her eyes, "I am sorry for doing that... I didn't mean to slap you so hard."

Normally, her soft, warm voice was enough to melt ice in

167

winter, yet now it was burning me like a magnifying glass. All I knew was that if Susan had been right about me, then what I said next was ultimately correct about her.

She added, and I must say 'soulfully', "I had no choice…"

"No choice?" I was still rubbing the sting from my left cheek and eye. "That is your problem, Susan. You exist in utter contempt of your free will." My face seriously hurt. She had a good right arm, even in her condition. "You always have a choice. You're problem is that you want someone else to make your choices for you."

*   *   *   *   *

July should mean, "Keeps getting hotter" and it would if our ancestors had chosen an Indian word instead of one derived from the romance languages to name it.

*   *   *   *   *

After a few moments standing on that trail, Susan turned to me and moved in closer, "Hug me and let's forgive one another."

"No. We can't."

"John…"

She stepped in a little bit closer then. Even unbearably thin, she looked magnificently beautiful, and all I could think about was how much I wanted to hold her in my arms, to feel her form, the contours of her shoulders, and her back beneath my hands. I longed for her warmth, to experience the sensation of knowing how much of a comfort we were to each other. I wanted finally to see how well we fit together, even standing, even clothed, but I could not. I could not bring myself to open up that dangerous door in good conscience.

Why? Because it was a gateway.

A little closer, then she said, "John, please… it's alright. Just hold me."

The problem was not in holding a beloved Christian Sister. The true problem existed between her and me.

* * * * *

Anger is the summer's sun, and anger leads to lust.

* * * * *

What I had seen repeatedly, and then once again on that July afternoon, was exactly what Susan Watts really wanted from me. What Susan wanted was to open the door to the possible solution to all of her problems. The thing was though; Susan wanted to feel her way to her conclusion. Rather than make the choice, rather than use her heart and mind and make an honest decision, she wanted to wade her way into the waters, never once admitting her intent. In this way, she could feign innocence.

Susan Watts was as guilty as I was.

* * * * *

Summer comes on slowly, but when it finally arrives, there is no mistaking it is there, and there is no turning back.

* * * * *

What Susan knew, and I truly believe this, is that if we were to embrace and began hugging, neither one of us would ever want to let go. Yet, she did not want to trust this knowledge. She wanted to prove it to herself before arriving at that conclusion. She wanted the opportunity to hold on to what she had while trying out something new.

She was cowardly.

She also knew that if she liked holding me, and hugging me, that such an embrace would invariably lead to our first kiss. Then she would have earned a partner in crime, someone to aid her in making her decision.

Susan was a coward and could not do it on her own. This is why she had to blame me for thinking exactly what she had been thinking all along.

If we had kissed, she would have then most likely sealed our commitment to the crime, by sleeping with me. In this way, she would create a situation in which there was no turning back.

That is how cowards achieve things.

What she did not want to accept, and what I had already accepted, was that there would never be a chance for us to escape the fact that we had initiated our love illicitly, and the price of that transgression would have been that our future together would not be blessed. All forgiveness aside, there is no escaping the consequences of breaking the laws of God.

There was also the slim chance that all she really wanted to do was to take a dip in order to test the waters; to see firsthand how her mind, heart, and body would react. If that was the case, and she was willing to risk it all for just one morsel, then it was I who risked being left out in the cold.

But I wasn't ready or willing to go back to that sort of darkness. Once saved, I would not allow myself to ever make that particular mistake again.

We live and learn.

Perhaps I was a coward as well.

* * * * *

Summer is the season set aside for watching water.

We are water watchers.

Fascinated by the ways in which water moves, and how it moves us, and how its motions soothe, we seek it out.

We watch water because it makes us feel that much more alive.

* * * * *

Susan moved in even closer to me then, and as I watched, she placed her hand upon my hip. When she touched my side, I quivered as the electricity of her touch ran steadily through me, strongly desiring her forbidden flesh. The temptation was painful, yet I enjoyed it for a moment.

170

I could almost feel Satan himself whispering his instructions as to how I should proceed to kiss her then.

* * * * *

Summer has the power to sweep us all away so easily... like an undertow at the beach, or the swiftly flowing current of a burgeoning stream beneath the storm.

* * * * *

Her face was no more than six inches from mine, and the natural fragrance of her hair and breath were hypnotizing. She wore no perfume... it was simply her body. Her lips looked so soft and inviting I could almost taste them as she spoke to me.

"I only want you to hold me, nothing more..."

She looked up into my eyes, and when she did, she placed her other hand upon my other hip. It was excruciatingly enticing to me.

"We're in the middle of nowhere... up here on this mountain, and there is nothing wrong with what we are doing and no one will ever know."

Just then, a shotgun blast rang out through the forest right behind us. Susan and I hit the ground so quickly we almost knocked each other's teeth out on the way down.

* * * * *

Summertime has long been viewed as the time of fireflies, fools, and simmering, smoldering, passionate madness beneath the Sun and the stars and the Moon.

* * * * *

The shot was not meant for us. It was just some kids shooting at cans out in the forest.

Either way, I took it as a sign for us to move on.

I think we both did.

* * * * *

Summertime is a wonderful time to pay attention to all that surrounds us.

* * * * *

August was another tricky month. Susan had not gained any weight for many weeks, and her "anemia" was getting worse.

Susan was getting nosebleeds almost daily, and she was starting to get scared. Although no matter what I said to her, she would not return to the doctor. She even began to hide her nosebleeds from me.

Marvin hardly ever came home on the weekends anymore, and this allowed for Susan and me to spend a lot of time alone. The only bad part of all that, as far as I was concerned, was that the entire congregation had begun talking.

Despite the gossip, we continued to have our innocent fun. My feelings on the subject were; as long as my association with Susan did not upset Marvin, then there was no reason for me to feel as if I had committed any sin. We flirted with disaster on a regular basis, but I never gave in to temptation.

Susan and I finally reached an awkward understanding. I would not engage in any adulterous act, and she would not admit that I was really what she wanted. We did not openly say these things, they just were.

Susan would never leave Marvin, so, we had reached a permanent impasse as neither one of us would ever break our rules.

That is, just as long as I never held her.

* * * * *

Spring is like a rattlesnake waiting in the grass.

* * * * *

The worst mistake I ever made in my life was to ignore the

word of God.

So, when God told me, "This is just who Susan is right now. This is where she is in her development and in her walk with me. Work with her as she *is* instead of wishing she were someone else or something different."

When God said this to me, I shut up and I listened.

* * * * *

Summer is like an old man waxing young.

* * * * *

The second biggest mistake I have ever made was to forget that life is a reflection of all that is inside of us. What I say to others, is what I most need to hear. The advice I give to others; the advice I need to take. The song I sing to others; the song I need to hear. All the many prayers I pray for others...

I told Susan that she was always turning away from the 'here and now' because she couldn't face the present, and that she would rather deal with all the many tomorrows and all the yesterdays because they were so much softer and easier to handle than today. I can now see that it was I who was always afraid of the moment. I was afraid of the consequences, even as much as she was, and I just kept putting off the inevitable while making up excuses for what I would and would not do. We played a spiritually romantic version of pass-the-buck and hot potato, and she was always the reflection of me, as I was in turn for her.

That was my greatest mistake and I could never see it. She was nearing death. I had the power to save her from the beginning. Instead, I kept on telling her to go first because I did not want to be wrong.

Or was that her charge since she was the one already married?

I may never know.

* * * * *

Summer can be a time of testing, even though school is out.

* * * * *

Susan had accepted a position working with the summer school program at the local elementary. She worked part time, five days a week, which left us with plenty of time to horse around. Two weeks into the summer program, a pervert showed up.

Back then, we simply called them perverts. They were not called pedophiles or child predators. There was no other definition; they were simply perverts.

This particular pervert had taken a liking to young boys.

Susan found him in the boy's lavatory attempting to manipulate one of her students into partaking in some form of sexually abstract entertainment. It was ugly. Susan did not know what to do, at first. I never got all the details.

Like I said, it was ugly.

It took all Susan had not to kill the perverted stranger, but in the end, all she managed to do was to protect the child and shoo the man off.

The totality of the occurrence did not fully hit her until later that afternoon.

Who did she run to?

She ran to me.

* * * * *

Autumn is a chance to get that child who is having trouble with their homework to know that you are the one person who believes that they are doing a very good job. With patience, reinforcement, and with time and understanding, they will do a very good job.

* * * * *

Susan had a look on her face unmatched by a rabid,

174

ravenous dog, even on its worst day. Susan, as I was when at first I heard the story, was prepared to kill or die for those little kids.

* * * * *

I have an issue with autumn: It forces us to realize we have equal portions of faith and doubt.

Summer is like a lover who is just about to break up with you… and then the breakup comes.

* * * * *

"For blessings counted and uncounted, forgiveness given and received, and for all the sins I can recall and for those that I cannot."

Susan said this prayer to me just before Thanksgiving, 1974.

"Have you ever done anything wrong? If you have, do you think it ever left you? Does it affect you?"

That is the reason why we pray such things to heaven.

* * * * *

Autumn is the season of the beautyberry and the favored bittersweet.

* * * * *

"All I know is how to make them laugh, how to listen to them, and how to make love, no… I know how to have sex with them… What I need to know from you is: How does a man ultimately love a woman? One woman. How?"

We used to get into some very deep conversations about love.

* * * * *

Autumn reminds us that there is always room for a little

error. In love, there is always room.

* * * * *

"A car ride in anger can often lead to sin, whereas a walk in anger may lead to cooling off."

Susan was still in shock for many days after her encounter with the pervert. The depth of it all did not really hit her for some time.

By winter, she would say that her entire purpose in life, and why she had been born, was to save that one small child from the clutches of that one demon possessed man. She would say it with a sparkle in her eye, knowing wholeheartedly that she had fulfilled her purpose in life. She would speak the words with a great sense of worth, value, gratitude, and faith; thankful that she finally knew why she had been born and why she had suffered so many, many ills before the end.

Susan would speak to me of this with everything... everything in her voice but pride.

* * * * *

Spring is a time for Easter eggs, crocus blossoms, putting up and dusting off the swing. Summer is a season never ending with its joys. Autumn, some claim, is but time spent preparing for winter. It is the time of harvest, when we reap the fruits of all the seeds that we have sown.

Winter is the colorful glow of Christmas lights on the bushes, frosted beneath winter's sweet blanket of precious, blue-white snow.

* * * * *

"Come down to me... and say that you love me." I used to practice this little song on the front porch of my cottage on the church property, just me with my guitar. It was a song written by Robinson Treacher about unrequited love.

I do not know if he ever sang it as solemnly as I did back

then.

* * * * *

Autumn is the perfect time for glowing pumpkins with all their toothy smiles. Autumn is the time when flowers die...

* * * * *

The last straw for Susan was that pervert showing up at the summer program at the elementary school that year. Although the memory gave purpose to her otherwise confusing and emotionally battered existence, the experience itself all but broke her in two.

While in shock, she nearly lost her faith in Christ Jesus. While recovering, she physically slipped into a terrible decline.

Although her eyes remained bright, her coloring began to fade. She faded almost consistently through until December. She continued to lose weight. By the end, she weighed close to nearly nothing at all.

First, there was Marvin's infidelity, proof of which Susan received when she saw them driving through town while in the car she had borrowed from her cousin when Marvin began to refuse her rides. Then there was his pervasive absence. Next came the news of Teesha's pregnancy, and then came a pervert to prey on her little ones at school.

Years before all this, there was a rainy Thursday evening when young Susan, still in grade school, sat at home alone thinking that her mother had deserted her as her father once had, leaving them for good. Then came the Friday morning when she found out her mother was dead. Later, and I did not know this until after Susan was admitted into the hospital, there came a striking case of Tuberculosis, which she had contacted from one of her johns the year she spent selling her body for cash. Then came a marriage to Marvin, and then came me...

The girl carried a tremendous burden of bricks in her wicker

177

basket.

* * * * *

The only way to know for sure that summer has transitioned into autumn, is that it suddenly grows cold.

* * * * *

Susan used to laugh whenever I was smiling. She used to say I smiled like a man who might get yelled at for smiling, but by whom she would never say.

* * * * *

Autumn can sometimes feel like the space after dinner between dessert time and bedtime, back when you were barely eight years old.

* * * * *

Susan used to say I had the type of arms that a woman would find appealing. She said that when a woman sees a pair of arms such as mine, she has only one desire, and that is to be held by them, securely.

Once, after a glass of wine and some tiramisu, she even referred to me as "Adorable."

* * * * *

Autumn is a time for drying flowers and saving their seeds. However, for Susan, summertime was not quite over, not quite yet.

* * * * *

By the Fourth of July, Susan was no longer in shock over the pervert incident and she was back to living with the rest of the

178

world. Nearly everyone in town drove out to see the fireworks. Susan and I, since Marvin was out of town on Teesha business, went up into the mountains to watch the fireworks from above, and from afar.

The fireworks were spectacular. From our vantage point at the scenic overlook, we could see three displays going off all at once. There was Mercerville's, Blain's, and the Cohampton fire department's display, which turned out to be the best.

It is amazing what can happen when you just sit back and take in the view.

* * * * *

Summertime can feel as if it will last forever, sometimes.

* * * * *

After the fireworks, we drove home slowly. It was not until after midnight that we finally made it back to the church where Susan had parked her car.

There we sat for a whole other hour just talking about the redwood trees and how life would get better someday. Someday.

* * * * *

Summertime is a season for stretching moments into hours, hours into memories, and simple pleasures into dreams that may or may not come true.

* * * * *

I was 30 and single in 1974, and there was only one reason for that. That reason was that I had not yet met a single woman that ever viewed me as a person. Rather, all the women I had ever found would simply size me up... a paycheck, a bulge, someone to show off to their friends. Those types of women disgusted me.

179

I think Susan was the first woman to ever love me, and to like me, for who, not just what, I really am.

* * * * *

Summer is the perfect time for sandy feet and salty hair.

* * * * *

Susan was the type of woman who would always look out for another's best interests. If she noticed me turning my head in any particular woman's direction, she would do her best to create a scenario in which the two of us might meet. She would ask me about my day even while she was crying.

* * * * *

Summer is the perfect time of year to introduce small children to the wonders of the heavens after dark.

* * * * *

She would always butter bread for other people at the table.

* * * * *

August allows us all a chance to blow a wish from a dandelion's perfectly transparent pearl of fuzzy white.

* * * * *

Susan was the type of woman who would not hesitate to fix your collar or pluck a random thread from your shoulder simply out of concern. She could stop any infant or toddler from crying with her compassionate smile and laugh. She caused boys, both young and old, to blush at the sight of her acknowledgement.

Susan was a gift unto others. It is much too sad that she did

180

not return that gift unto herself.

* * * * *

August never rushes, although it seems to fly right by.

* * * * *

Susan was a picnic and a party, wrapped in a prairie skirt and summer blouse.

* * * * *

August provides a certain confirmation that we are still very much alive.

* * * * *

Susan could chose to become a child at any given moment.

* * * * *

August would have been the better choice as the very last month of any year.

* * * * *

We live our lives basing our observances of the passage of time on an agricultural calendar. We awake to cold at the New Year, waxing impatient for the tilling to begin. We sow, we water, we nurture, we wait... and then we harvest at the appropriate time, completing the cycle with our return to the darkness, unto the darkness and the long forgotten cold.
One year is the reflection of any given day.
Our calendar is the reflection of our lives.

* * * * *

Meeting Susan was a close second to meeting my personal savior, the savior I had found in Jesus Christ. Her laughter blessed me, her countenance freed me, and her promise filled me with so much love and delight that otherwise, not having found her; I might have merely waded through this life, always avoiding the deep. She showed me that my eyes really could be opened wider. Knowing her was my very first lesson in truly being gentle with another life.

* * * * *

If spring is like hair, and summer like legs, then winter must be the closing of eyes, and autumn the wistful fragrance of all four season's sweet perfume.

* * * * *

Susan had managed to kiss me in the graveyard, but only once.

* * * * *

Autumn is always just around the corner, and winter is just a school day away.

* * * * *

We met back in 1973 while the war in Vietnam was finally coming to an end. We were both Christians, and both of us detested the war. She and I met on August 28th that year. I fell in love with her sometime before though, the moment I set eyes on her. I had no idea that she was married, back then.
Now I may just spend the rest of my lifetime sorting that out.

* * * * *

September first can often feel sadder than removing your

combination lock from your locker on the very last day of school.

* * * * *

Susan used to love to flip her long curly hair when we were talking.

* * * * *

September feels like someone is pushing you forward from behind.

* * * * *

Curly.
That is what I used to call her when we first met.
Curly.
She had a head of hair that could have sold shampoo.
Curly…
It was a terrible thing to watch the cancer take that hair.
Then she was gone.

* * * * *

September is like a big, tan rubber band sitting on a table just waiting for someone to play with it.

* * * * *

Sometimes I would call her Sparkles. I would call her that because of the way her eyes would twinkle when she would look at me. Susan always thought it had something to do with the rhinestones on her jeans.

Susan's mind was always on fire in the same way in which an opal stone or autumn leaves could be said to have fire; her mind was bursting with color, effervescently exploding like a watercolor painting sprinkled with light.

She was so captivating back then, even until the very end.

* * * * *

Autumn is discovering that path that leads to nowhere through the woods.

* * * * *

I have always felt that the true test of beauty is to close your eyes while a person is talking and then see if that person appears just as beautiful to you in the dark.

* * * * *

September first is like a piece of bubble-wrap just waiting to be popped and snapped between your fingers.

* * * * *

We watched every sunrise together during the month of September, 1974. Susan would drive out in the dark after Marvin had left for work, if he had even come home, and sometimes we would share coffee.

* * * * *

September first is like a young girl on a first date just waiting for that very first kiss.

* * * * *

"Have you ever seen a sunrise in the rain?"
"I did not think you could see the sunrise while it is raining."
"Sometimes you can."
A sunrise in the rain was another one of those things I had somehow missed out on. I had never once seen a butterfly emerge from its cocoon, yet Susan claimed to have seen this on more than one occasion in the wild. I had never seen a shooting star during the sunset, yet Susan had. I had also never

184

once witnessed a leaf actually break away from a tree in the fall, yet Susan had seen all of these things and more. I had never watched the grass grow, a snowfall come to an end, nor spy on an icicle as it formed. I had never seen a hummingbird hover, or a snake disappear into a hole.

There were dozens of experiences that many others claimed to have had, that have always eluded me.

What the rest of the world was unaware of though, was that I was the fortunate observer blessed enough to have seen Susan's eyes sparkle majestically and mystically on so many more occasions than anyone else in the world.

* * * * *

Cool September evenings are akin to a large, slow glass of deep red wine.

* * * * *

Susan first began to cough up blood on a Sunday afternoon.

* * * * *

September is full of gentle rubies in the dark.

* * * * *

Susan first began to cough up blood on a Sunday afternoon. The date was September 12, 1974. Marvin had not shown up for church in four months. We had no idea what could have caused Susan to cough up so much blood, and it came as a very horrifying surprise for all concerned. She was so young.

Not one of us would have ever imagined cancer.

* * * * *

Life holds a brilliant assortment of crimson berries in the fall.

185

* * * * *

I can still remember the day Susan told me that each of our souls is like an arrow.

She was in the hospital.

She said that our entire lives are spent pulling back on the bow, and that it is very important for each and every arrow to be aimed directly at Heaven before we die, when our arrows are finally released.

* * * * *

The frost of late November comes on quicker and colder than death.

* * * * *

With the first frost of autumn comes the chill, and with that chill; the flowers, darkened and withered, shrivel temporarily and then begin to dry. Susan's cough began to worsen and eventually she began to take on the habit of sleeping in late. She was not sad, she was simply tired. Not depressed, it was just that she was running out of time.

* * * * *

The whole world changes when it rains. No longer is the sky a cheerful blue. No longer is the air a gentle kiss. When it rains in mid October, something about the mind numbing reflections in the puddles of the streetscape drive us to contemplate a smaller, darker world... to shiver at the prospect that most of us will never make it to all the places we have ever wished to go.

Susan used to hand me small bits of folded paper on which she had carefully written Bible quotes for me. My favorites came from Ecclesiastes and Proverbs, and from the many books of Kings.

I saved every one of those random bits of paper in a shoebox under my bed. They were all handwritten, every single one of them with love.

* * * * *

Autumn is the stillness of the fading spots upon a fawn in early morning.

* * * * *

On October 8, 1974, I found a small maple leaf, red, with its veins outlined in fiery streaks of orange-yellow. I sealed it in an envelope and gave it to Susan in the foyer of our old, stone chapel. When she opened it, she cried.

* * * * *

Autumn, for some, is goodnight.

* * * * *

I told her that the leaf reminded me of a person. The leaf had five lobes, like the arms, legs, and head of a human body with the fire of the Holy Spirit brightly burning deep within.
Susan said the leaf was just one of God's daily miracles.
With this, I gently agreed.

* * * * *

How it is that that the cold never threatens the crocus and chrysanthemums in the autumn and the spring?

* * * * *

Susan wrote me a letter on October 15th that described to me how much my leaf had affected her. She wrote how she had gone for a walk that morning only to observe hundreds of individual examples of how God can make a universe within the surface of a leaf. How God can take the time to paint each one separately. How nature compliments a seemingly endless pallet with inexhaustible creativity and how we are granted the right... how we are granted the right to walk amongst the foliage as it falls. She claimed that this alone was one of God's greatest gifts to us.

She signed the letter, "Love, Susan" and her signature entered my soul through my eyes, and then within my chest her dying words began to hurt me.

It was on that day that I finally realized that I had been granted the right to walk in Susan's presence by Almighty God.

* * * * *

October is a terrible time to suspect that a loved one may in fact be dying.

* * * * *

Susan had to quit her job working with the children because she could no longer manage to make it out of bed on time to get to the school in the morning. She attributed it all to her husband's indiscretions and how they made her feel.

And so did I... until I saw the blood.

* * * * *

The rains of autumn always seem to fall straight down.

* * * * *

She handled her dilemma by volunteering with the children every other afternoon or so; whatever she could handle at the time. Her first day back with the children after spending nearly a week away was rough on her. Some of the children asked her if the reason she had not said goodbye was that she no longer liked them.

No words can describe the form of tears that Susan cried that day.

* * * * *

A chilly, wet autumn evening... there is something about the way in which streetlights cast their glow, elongated and stringent, yet vibrantly along the wet and soggy avenue. Something about the sound of wet rubber against pavement as the cars roll by. There is something about the silence when the rain stops, the way the darkened images amidst the shadows just seem to carry on like ghosts in gloom.

The sound of Susan's voice was one of the greatest gifts I have ever received, and I am fortunate to have found her.

* * * * *

Autumn is the perfect time of year to say goodbye.

* * * * *

My work around the church never ended. Mid-October meant there was plenty of wood needed and once again, I was out in the woods, alone. It was me alone with the scavenging chipmunks and the smell of dampening mushroom wood. Me alone with God and His forest. Me alone with the truth.

The truth was that I was in love with Susan, and that was a terrible thing and I had to admit that to God. I was in love with her face, her body, her personality, her spirit... her dying body and her living soul.

I repented that day in the woods, and every day thereafter.

* * * * *

Autumn is a time for reconciling with one's own reflection.

* * * * *

Moss, lichens, mushrooms, trailing cedar... rotten logs covered in shelf fungi, falling leaves, and fallen leaves of old. Latent songbirds, breezes, thin streams of the clearest water trickling down through the earth over time tested stone.

* * * * *

Susan was an angel in disguise.

* * * * *

Breathe in deeply the fragrance of the forest. Turn over salamander stones and smell the forgotten earth you will find there, beneath.

Autumn is the holy reminder of our great impermanence as living beings.

* * * * *

Susan was a woman who never stopped believing.

* * * * *

Pick up a stone, any stone; the one that catches your eye. Throw it mightily out into the forest. Then, standing calmly, reckon with your perfect limitations.

* * * * *

Susan had been hiding the fact that she had been coughing up blood. The horror she experienced upon first noticing the red... the small yet bright and rutilant specks on the tissue forced her to retreat into a silent vow of feigning courage. Then the blood began to come on stronger over the next few weeks. She was lost and afraid, alone, and she tried to blame it all away on stress.

* * * * *

Autumn is the season when all the faithful leaves may retire into Heaven, a Heaven rest assured for every family tree.

* * * * *

Sam Barnett donated a brand-new 28-inch chainsaw to the church just before Halloween that year. He owned the only hardware store in town, and he was truly a cheerful giver. He delivered the chainsaw with a gallon of gasoline, and a gallon of bar/chain oil.

Sam Barnett was a masterful man, and he made my life much easier. For Sam Barnett, I will also always be grateful.

* * * * *

Autumn comes on slowly, daring us to let go of the ever greening past of our sweet memories, so we might better understand and accept the here and now.

* * * * *

Covered in sawdust and bar/chain oil, I smiled when Susan's car arrived in the lot. She was wearing a blue and white dress, white stockings, and tan leather boots. However, my smile shattered into an expression of horrified concern when I saw her walking towards me. There was crimson blood and browner blood all over her long, right sleeve.

* * * * *

No one ever tells you what it is like to watch a friend die. No one ever tells us when we are young that we may one day have to offer them that particular friendly hand, a hand they might hold onto, a hand that keeps the trembling cold of death at bay.

No one ever tells us what it will be like to watch a good friend cry; knowing sincerely in our hearts there is precious little left to say.

* * * * *

Autumn is like the perfect apple pie. Autumn is a steaming raspberry muffin. It is a beautiful season, replete with sweetness and promise, bursting with expectation in the crisp mountain air, and then there are always the colorful leaves.

* * * * *

She walked across the parking lot towards my truck with a marble-white look upon her face. I had never once seen her eyes looking so sharply blue than before that moment. There was a little blood on her hand, but mostly it was on her steering wheel. The rest was on her right sleeve from where she had wiped her lips.

She was dying.

We both recognized this immediately.

It was right before our eyes.

I could not move.

* * * * *

Autumn is the perfect time to lie in the grass and just listen.

* * * * *

I placed the chainsaw down on the gate of my truck. When the feeling returned to me, I prayed she would not fall. Even from across the parking lot, I could tell how panicked she was and how labored her breathing had become. Wanting to run to her and hold her then, I had to fight all my urges; I simply picked up a rag and began to clean off my hands.

By the time Susan made it to the rear end of my pickup, and to my side, she had already made the decision to cover her right hand with her left.

This was an unnecessary attempt to hide what she considered shame.

* * * * *

Autumn knows of colors of which you may not be aware.

* * * * *

Her hands were trembling frightfully and her face was white as a linen sheet. Her eyes were glittery, yet glossy and red, blue as an eagle's as she stared. Her hair was a mess, yet she still looked quite beautiful to me.

That is when I noticed how deeply red and altogether terrifying some forms of blood can be.

* * * * *

Autumn fights for space within the room of our appreciation, while so many simply sit and complain about the onset of the cold.

* * * * *

Susan's favorite expression of life was always the crimson berries of the fall. We know them as beautyberry, hew berries, bittersweet, cotoneaster, hawthorn, holly, and the winterberry sprigs. Susan knew the names of each of these, but she chose to lump them into one big succulent, yet inedible category: the crimson berries of the fall. She claimed they always made her wish that she could be born again as a bird whenever she spied a cluster peeking out through the shivering snow.

* * * * *

Autumn is God's invisible blanket, which tells the forest and its inhabitants that it is time to go to sleep.

* * * * *

I had no idea what to say. I found myself wandering through

thoughts of great concern for her condition. The blood on her sleeve was beginning to dry, but her eyes were beginning to wet.

I could not hold her. I could not offer her a hug.

* * * * *

The colors of autumn have taught me two wonderful things. One is that there is no limit to God's imagination.

* * * * *

Together we stood there in the blinding sunshine of the parking lot with the church's old stone walls as a backdrop to our fate.

Marvin was out of town, as usual, tending to his girlfriend and their unborn child. I was the surrogate manhood, at a distance, coldly, desperate and afar. While Marvin was laughing with his woman, Susan was screaming for mercy through the silence of her forever burning tears.

* * * * *

Autumn drops her silvery dew upon the forest floor, performing endlessly in her magical wilderness, dancing the slowest waltz one might ever hope to see.

* * * * *

Susan had not slept nor had she eaten any solid food for over twenty-four hours. She told me her cough was so violent she could not keep anything down or get any rest. She coughed again, and the shiniest of red blood appeared like a whisper of death upon her lips then.

* * * * *

Autumn is a weeping sunflower drying alone in a field.

Autumn is a paper airplane released from a child's soft hand. Autumn is an angel... an angel waiting to land.

* * * * *

Susan's eyes became erratic then, as if her soul had finally, and ultimately, been awakened abruptly from its sleep.

* * * * *

Autumn is the nectar that only God can wring from a year.

* * * * *

The sunlight struck her face so perfectly that her eyes became at once a most mystifying blue and brilliant.
Neither one of us had spoken a word yet, nor could we speak just then.

* * * * *

Autumn is like money lent, which only once forgotten, might return.

* * * * *

Susan looked like one of God's soldiers, a warrior in shambles, wounded on the battlefield of trust and love and lies.

* * * * *

October holds within its name many haunting expressions of night, of sumptuousness and truest delights. The apples come pouring in by the bushel full, glossed and shiny, plumped up with sugary juice. The cornstalks dry, the pumpkins harden to perfection, and a bowl of chicken corn chowder never has tasted so good. There is a certain unseen pressure that arrives with the month of October that drives us to live more thoroughly.

Susan's heartbeat began to grow faster.

*　*　*　*　*

Autumn is a great time of year to simply find yourself standing by the roadside, or by the wayside, or on any path, all alone, standing in awe of all that God has ever done.

*　*　*　*　*

Susan's eyes widened in accord with my own, wider than any eyes I had ever seen. Then she lifted her hand and wiped the thin layer of blood from her mouth.

*　*　*　*　*

Autumn is the perfect time to speak in whispers.

*　*　*　*　*

As she lowered her hand, we could both see the blood there. There was no denying or mistaking what it was.

*　*　*　*　*

Autumn is the time of the great, elastic fermentation. The scents you adore, as you smell the autumn leaves; the scent of the forest, the scent of the dampening earth, even the scent of freshly baked bread – all these fragrances are enhanced by alcohol – one of the primary results of fermentation and of yeast.

In autumn, nature is a brew master. The forest becomes her winery, with all the twigs, nuts, husks, leaves, grains, and berries ground up and tossed into the mix. Then, as all the merry creatures of the earth become lightly intoxicated by her tannic juices and subtly influential nectars, they lay themselves to rest beneath the pines and prepare for bed.

* * * * *

I picked Susan a bouquet of chrysanthemums from my garden behind the church. Strange how one can get all caught up in the change of seasons only to forget that there are still flowers left to share.

* * * * *

The richest black earth is born in autumn.

* * * * *

There she stood by the open bed of the truck. I will never forget that day, although I have tried. Both Susan and I first reckoned with our mortality that day.

The sight of blood had never before posed such an imminent threat to me. She was my friend, my dear, dear friend – a love of mine – and she was lost and frightened beyond any degree, desperately in search of some way in which to affix her faith to the situation as she wiped the blood from her hand.

I couldn't hold her… I did not dare.

We walked indoors and prayed together, and then I drove her to the hospital and waited while she sat and received the first of her bad news.

* * * * *

In autumn, you can look up at the starry sky and invent your own constellations… if you choose to.

* * * * *

The doctors gave Susan one month to live.

The attending physician asked me, as her friend, to join them in his office after her examination was complete. His office was a very sad room. There was little more than dark wood, dark carpeting, dark leather furniture, and the dark, barren spines of the many thick books he kept there. It reminded me of an oversized casket with a window, a plant, and a desk.

There I learned that Susan had suffered from tuberculosis as a young adult, and that, coupled with her long habit of smoking, had led to the predicament she found herself in.

I could do nothing except to pray. Susan Watts was really dying.

* * * * *

There are scarier monsters contained within this fragile existence than all the ghosts and goblins of an October's moon combined.

* * * * *

I enquired about treatment. The doctor informed us that each of her lungs had been thoroughly overtaken, and her cancer, along with her earlier scarring, had led to the condition she was in.

"Susan is experiencing what used to be referred to as *consumption*."

She was literally withering away.

* * * * *

Autumn is an oak leaf soaked in blood.

* * * * *

How does death choose its victims?

When I was a child, they told us that God takes us when we have completed our tasks here on Earth. Presumably, this is precisely the time when our services are required in Heaven. I always liked that explanation; it made sense in a comforting way. Later I learned that not every soul gets into Heaven, and that one fact caused me to turn my eyes to the Lord.

Horrifically, my eyes returned to Susan's in that dreaded casket of a room.

* * * * *

Winter is the spider's web rarely unattended. Autumn is the unassuming fly.

* * * * *

When Susan and I first met, I thought I had fallen in love with her.

* * * * *

Autumn is a daisy drying upright in a field. Autumn is the pokeweed berry's ink.

* * * * *

I had no idea what love really was back then. Walking down that long, cold hallway with Susan beside me, I felt my heart breaking like a tree struck by lightning in an open, empty field. I was the oak split in two, and then suddenly, if not miraculously, I discovered the meaning of love.

* * * * *

Autumn is the immaculate absence of birdsong in the clear of the one forgotten day.

* * * * *

When I was a child, I prayed for miracles like a rocket ship in my backyard. On schooldays, I would pray for a hundred feet of snow. Walking out of the hospital that day, I looked up to the sky and asked God to grant Susan another 25 years.

I even told Him He could take them from me, if that would be alright.

* * * * *

Autumn is the Canada Geese spelling out "goodbye" in a language consisting of nothing but "V's" and "W's."

* * * * *

I told God He could take 25 years away from me. However, I did not like the answer I received.

* * * * *

Autumn makes the trees around the lake begin to shiver.

* * * * *

Susan washed down her first morphine pill along with her chemical medicines with a paper cup full of water from the silver spigot that bent like a swan's long neck over the doctor's sink. The doctor had told her that treatment would be fruitless, and that she would lose her hair, but I convinced her to take the medication anyhow.

It was all we really had aside from prayer.

* * * * *

Autumn is like a ladybird beetle turning into a tiny red stone.

* * * * *

Susan was still in shock when I stopped at a payphone. The tears had not yet begun to flow from her pale white face just then. We were both in shock.

We drove out to the diner for a bite to eat, although Susan found it hard to try to make it through a handful of French fries. I ordered us each a chocolate malted. She drank most of that.

Afterwards, we drove back to the church to meet with pastor. He was standing outside in the parking lot when we arrived.

* * * * *

Autumn is a walk outside when no one else is watching. Autumn takes its time to laugh out loud. Autumn is breakfast and autumn is lunch. Autumn is the difference between a sure thing and a hunch. Autumn is the smile of a child who is growing.

Autumn is a poem written on a leaf.

Autumn is a giver, whereas winter is a thief.

* * * * *

I let pastor take Susan for a walk while I went inside to stoke the fire.

* * * * *

Autumn is a billion elderly children turning around to look at the past while wishing there was more.

* * * * *

When I arrived by the furnace in the basement of the church, I fell against the wall and broke down hard. I grit my teeth to hold back the things I really wanted to say to God while I was down there. And then I screamed so hard at the foundation, that I thought the church might fall.

* * * * *

There is rarely ever such a thing as a third chance at getting things right. Autumn is a time for second chances.

*　*　*　*　*

The Bible tells us that love is patient, love is kind, love understands, is never quick to anger or slight of tongue. Faced with losing everything I had ever loved beneath my Lord and Savior, thoughts of *love* had all but devastated me then.

The basement of the church smelled of stone, and dust, and ashes.

*　*　*　*　*

Autumn's heart weeps within the weathered willows.

*　*　*　*　*

I do not know if it was facing death that brought this on, or the morphine, or the chemo, but Susan began writing and she did not stop writing for nearly two months and then she died. She died on the first day of winter, December 21, 1974.

She wrote short poems about the things she loved; flowers, trees, belonging… and she wrote many, many lines about each one of the seasons; winter, spring, summer, and fall.

*　*　*　*　*

All four seasons are a pinwheel spinning 'round.

*　*　*　*　*

Some of her poems were beautiful and simple. Others, many of them, I did not fully understand nor can I appreciate, but perhaps that is only because I am not yet at death's door.

*　*　*　*　*

Autumn is the sandstone upon which the blue snake of a sky sheds its crackling skin as patterned clouds beneath the Sun.

202

* * * * *

I cried harder than I had ever cried before in my life down there in the church's basement by the furnace, and all I could think about was Susan, and Marvin, and Teesha Daniels, and sin. I thought about a month's worth of time, and how short a span of time that really is, and how many opportunities had slipped by during which I could have truly loved and honored Susan.

Had I been mistaken? Should I have held her in my arms? Should I have kissed her and broken Marvin's wicked spell? Should I have been the one to give her the strength, and likewise the reason, for her to walk away? Would things have turned out differently if I had helped her to leave him the day she discovered his infidelity? Would we have had a chance?

Would the cancer have stayed away?

If I had had the guts to change things... would she have lived?

* * * * *

Autumn is the perfect time to put aside childish things.

* * * * *

Who can measure love but God above us? Who is to say I did the right thing or the wrong? God tells us that no person should come between a man and a woman once joined together by Him, and that the only good reason for divorce is infidelity.

On the day that I saw Marvin's Caprice rocking by the bridge that traversed Mulley Creek, I had found the inclination and the justification to seduce Susan along with the excuse for her to leave him.

Should I have told her what I saw? Should I have kissed her once, and then saved the rest for marriage? Would she have left him if I opened up that door?

* * * * *

Autumn is the time for heavy questions and heavenly answers.

* * * * *

If love is truly above all things, then should I have run straight to her, knowing what I had known, and told her of Marvin's indiscretion, and begged for her hand?

* * * * *

Autumn is a box of crayons melting slowly over trees.

* * * * *

I tried to load wood into the furnace, but each piece of wood I picked from the stack felt like a pound of sin and a pound of flesh laid before the judgment seat of God. I was a tortured soul, burning in the cellar, dying inside, knowing that God would not take me in her place.
I begged Him.
I begged Him.
I begged of Him.
And then I screamed.

* * * * *

Autumn is a child asking questions about sleep and dreams.

* * * * *

My arms felt so heavy it was as if they were made out of lead, and every piece of wood I attempted to place upon the dying embers within the furnace felt as if it were a piece of me that I could not let go of. I recalled the words Susan had spoken to me in that cellar room so long ago during the last winter's snowstorm, how she had begged me just to welcome her into my arms when she was still so young, alive, and so well. I could recall that I did not want to risk temptation and felt damned for having blamed over half of it on her.

I was half the man I used to be.

I fell to my knees on the hard dirt floor and I stared into the furnace, wanting nothing more than to burn myself alive for my awkward misdeeds.

* * * * *

Autumn reminds us that Jesus willingly traded places with Barabbas, a murderer... in order to hang between two thieves upon the cross.

How Barabbas must be singing joyfully for all eternity for having been the first to have been saved by him.

How sweet the tears of Barabbas must fall.

* * * * *

A week before Susan died; she told me that she had received a vision of what was to come. She told me that she now believed that God Himself would show her all the many paths her life may have taken, if only she had made the other choice.

* * * * *

Autumn is the lullaby sung in every key.

* * * * *

When her walk with Pastor was complete, the three of us sat in the sanctuary and prayed together for Susan's health. We were asking for a miracle, but the three of us knew she was already gone.

What she received was one extra month than they had given her.

* * * * *

Autumn is a time for make-believe.

* * * * *

Later that fall, the doctors had given Susan two options; she could admit herself into the hospital, or die at home. After considering the thought of spending a month at home alone without Marvin, or even with Marvin, she told us that she would like to admit herself to the hospital and spend the rest of her time there.

I offered to allow her to finish out her time with me at my cottage, but she told me that it would be terribly inappropriate for her to stay there.

She cited three good reasons, and I reluctantly agreed. The first was the Father, the second was the Son, and the third was the Holy Ghost.

Then she told the doctor she wanted one last day outside...

* * * * *

Autumn slows things down and speeds things up at the very same time.

* * * * *

Susan asked me if I would take one last walk down to the pond with her that afternoon, and we did.

Across the dry, yellowing grasses of late October we walked, silently, each of us taking things in as if we both had barely one last month to live and breathe. She was sharing her awestruck bewilderment with me.

The sky above us was perfectly blue and perfectly white and it was all so refreshing. The changing leaves and all the many that had already changed and had fallen were like an audience of millions, each in the favorite seat, all acting as witnesses to our last walk to the waters of the terrifying baptism that was to come. We did not hold hands, yet we did walk very closely together.

To me it looked as if Susan was walking the plank.

* * * * *

Autumn captures us like fireflies within Earth's holy jar of light and clay.

* * * * *

We sat on the slope by the edge of the pond, watching as the colored leaves blew across its placid surface like ghostly images passing before the reflective mirror of our lives. Susan pointed into the stark reflection of the forest and told me that the red maple was her absolute favorite one.

* * * * *

Autumn is chock full of alternative endings...

* * * * *

Susan told me she did not want a burial in the ground. Then she asked me if I could be the one to scatter her ashes after she was gone.

I've never been one to cry too readily. Her words tore open a space within me that has not closed to this day. I could not think it. I could not bear to say it. But there were those words, *"After I am gone..."*

* * * * *

If springtime is a child first leaning to walk, then autumn is a spirit preparing to fly.

* * * * *

I had been trying hard until that very moment to be the stronger one, but I must admit that final "yes" was the most difficult word I have ever spoken.

"Yes," I would scatter her ashes, and I both hated her and loved her for asking me that.

* * * * *

Autumn is the seventh attempt to get your kite up off the ground, and the feeling you get while you frantically let out more line as it soars away.

* * * * *

Frozen within the permanence of the moment, too frozen to speak for a while, then Susan broke the silence by informing me that she would like to have her ashes scattered over the pond.

She said, "Then, whenever you go swimming, you could be swimming inside of me."

A thousand bolts of lightning flashed as the thunder slowly roared within me, and I could have crushed her then with my love for her if I had ever dared to try.

* * * * *

Autumn's truths are spoken softly, if ever at all.

* * * * *

Across the barren reaches of the space that was between us, I defied the law of God and took Susan's hand in mine.

* * * * *

Autumn is to fire what springtime is to ice.

* * * * *

I will never forget the look on Susan's face when I first took her hand in mine that day by the pond. The look on her face spoke volumes; some of the sentiments were lovingly positive, while still others spoke of something very wonderful and pure, yet altogether happening too late.

* * * * *

Autumn is a time of haunting winds and rustling leaves.
Autumn is the time of life when so many will dare to believe.

* * * * *

Her hand felt small in mine, fragile, bony, and tender; although younger, her hand felt older. Her fingers were frail and thin.

The sun felt somehow warmer upon our shoulders once joined in that way, and I truly feel that if it is at all possible that an autumn day can hold the vested power to join two souls in Holy Matrimony, that Susan and I were in some way married that day. I knew then in my heart, without a doubt; that no matter what became of Susan Watts, we would someday share eternity together in Heaven above.

* * * * *

Winter is to summer all that nighttime is to a day.

* * * * *

Susan's hospital stay was not unlike the stays of others on the floor of the intensive care unit. The room smelled of detergent and astringents, old people and bleach. The only thing that made those few short weeks tolerable was the look in Susan's eyes when I would walk through the doorway each morning and in the late of afternoon.

All she ever asked me for was some writing paper and pens. Her only request was that I would sit with her and from time to time hold her hand.

The nurses took very good care of her during her stay.

* * * * *

Winter is to sunlight what plate glass is to the rain.

* * * * *

Susan stopped eating on December 11, yet she continued to live on for ten more days.

* * * * *

Winter's heart is beating like a field mouse in the snow.

* * * * *

During her stay in ICU, Susan wrote nearly four hundred lines of poetry, some more beautiful than others. Some were sad, capturing the darkness and the quietude of the hospital like a small dark pond in autumn can capture the reflection of the trees. By the end, her handwriting was barely legible.

Although difficult, I managed to read and decipher them all.

It's all that I have left of her, aside from memories.

* * * * *

Winter is all of our lyrics set to music in the cold.

* * * * *

On one afternoon, Marvin showed up with flowers for Susan. I stepped outside for a smoke in order to leave them alone. Teesha Daniels was in the passenger's seat of his Caprice Classic, holding a baby in her arms.

Teesha and I acknowledged one another's presence, but that was all.

When I later returned to Susan's room, she was crying. She handed me the card Marvin had given her with the roses. It read, "Get well soon."

* * * * *

Winter is a strand of silver hair, blown upon the wind like the tinsel of a soul. Susan Watts would not see Christmas after all.

* * * * *

That evening the nurses and the doctors allowed me to stay all night in Susan's room. We mostly sat in silence, with me in a chair next to her bed, gently holding her hand. The date was December 20, 1974, five days before Christmas…

* * * * *

Winter is a twilight memory.

* * * * *

The day I met Susan Watts, she was dressed like a flower in full bloom.

* * * * *

Winter is the time of year when it is most difficult to tell the difference between a tree and its long cast shadow.

* * * * *

Susan was like a breeze that had entered the room upon someone failing to have closed the door properly behind them. Susan was a poem written by the hand of a skilled calligrapher. She was music silently resounding, played outdoors. Her hair was curly. Its color sable-brown, and a most gently tarnished forest gold.

Her eyes were blue.

Her heart was true.

And for the last day of her life, she was all mine.

* * * * *

Winter is the sound the angels make when they are sleeping.

* * * * *

The things that enter into and then pass through one's mind while they are sitting bedside watch for a friend in dire need often come on like echoing drumbeats from a past some might better view as lost and totally forgotten. You recall everything. It is the coldest seat in the world.

The first thing Susan wanted to know about me was whether I had ever seen God. Then she told me she thought that standing in the rain felt like receiving a very cool blessing, and with this, I agreed.

I was the first man to have the guts to tell her she was wrong. I was also the first man to speak advice she did not want, but knew she had to hear.

I think I was also the very first man to have ever truly fallen in love with every ounce of her being.

We shared her favorite dessert that day. We laughed out loud. We discovered that two people can fall in love without kissing. We smiled.

Later, we would walk for hours, sometimes carrying fresh milk from the farm next door. We chased after birds and feathers, and so much more.

Our struggle... our path together was one beset with rules, fair rules, the prying eyes of others, and the ever-watchful glance of God. For more reasons than I care to go into, there was no way we could have ever had a physical affair. I think we were deeply in love; I know we were deeply in love, more in love than most people ever will be, when you discount sexual trysts and all the romance.

Our love was like the love between two innocents before they reach an age or an allowance at which point they might sneak away to touch. Ours was a love existing within the guidelines of the Kingdom of Heaven; although I am quite sure we may have bent or even broken some of the rules.

*   *   *   *   *

Winter is a seashell no bare hand will ever touch.

*   *   *   *   *

Sitting by her side as she dozed in and out of her morphine induced confidences, I listened to the memories of both her laughter and her screams. There was a time when we once spent the afternoon tossing a football to one another. It was the most fun I had ever had with a woman in all my many years.

We were both dressed in flannel and denim, and her hair was long and it was a September day back in 1973 and the church lawn was green with acorns and the last of the dandelions. There were squirrels running everywhere.

Every time I caught the ball, Susan cheered for me, and every time Susan had, I would do the same.

*   *   *   *   *

Winter is your upside down reflection in the spoon.

*   *   *   *   *

The football was a gift from my cousin who played for UMASS. I got it on a Thursday in the mail and I taught Susan how to throw that Saturday afternoon.

That was the second weekend after Marvin had begun working for the church.

I did not know it then, but Susan had come to the sanctuary to pray because Marvin had not come home the night before. She did not mention this fact to me. She just showed up at the church and began talking about how lovely the autumn day was and how she had nothing else to do. I said, "It's that time of year… would you like to toss a ball?" No leaves had begun to fall yet, just the acorns.

She flexed her muscle to show me how strong she was and she said, "You betcha!" I had no idea then what I was doing for her on that lonesome autumn day.

* * * * *

Winter is the sound of toning bells.

* * * * *

They agreed to let me stay with Susan that night at the hospital because one of the nurses had overheard Marvin and Susan's conversation, and knowing quite well that he was her husband, and that he had not been around; they thought she probably should not be left alone for a while. I for one believe that God Himself must have spoken to that nurse that afternoon, because He was the only one that knew.

* * * * *

Winter is the sound of gently falling snow upon the water.

* * * * *

I knew Susan Watts for exactly 481 days, from August 28, 1973 until December 21, 1974. During that time, I watched her spirit torn apart as if by a pack of wolves, then picked by crows. When she died, she weighed less than 52 pounds.

* * * * *

Winter bears a light that shines across the darkness into forever, like a lighthouse trolls for wanderers from ashore.

* * * * *

Susan's death caused me to develop a theory. If we were purely physical beings, then doctors could probably heal anything and there would be no more concerns regarding health. If we were purely psychological beings, then psychologists could heal everyone from the onset, and no one would ever have to suffer from mental or physical illness again. If we were purely emotional beings, then love alone could probably solve every one of our ills.

The truth is, we are all physical, psychological, emotional, and spiritual beings, and the only thing that can truly fix us is God, our creator.

In a way, it is like sending something back to the manufacturer when it is broken. Unfortunately, for some, we do not heed the warning signs of malfunction and trouble. We do not take the time to read the owner's manual. We do not keep up with the recommended maintenance program, and we always wait to deal with things until after it is too late. When we do this, it leads to suffering and quite often death.

I now believe that sin can and will lead to premature death in human beings, however, it is not always *our own sin* that does this.

* * * * *

Autumn is a one-lane road that leads to everywhere and anywhere at all.

* * * * *

The pond behind our church was always full of fish.

When I say pond, I do not mean a very deep puddle. The pond behind our church was nearly a hundred yards wide and seventy yards to the very far side. Glacial retreat created the pond on the property long, long ago, some say, when a glacier retreated and left a deep hole. There are similar ponds all over the county. No one ever had to dig a pond in our hometown.

I used to enjoy spending mornings by the pond watching the mist lift off from its surface, along with the hatch, as largemouth bass stole away at their morning meals. The fishing was good, and so was the eating, and for the most part, the water was always quite clear. Some spots were deep, other spots deeper, seemingly bottomless at times. There were turtles there, and there were frogs.

In the wintertime, the pond would freeze over, and on some odd years, it was thick enough to skate on all winter long. I liked the way the snow crept down to the edge to meet the dark water… or eventually the ice.

In spring, the pond would slowly awaken and fill with signs of life again. Many creatures would lay their eggs there, and strange new birds, and many familiar, would all come around.

In the summertime, the dragonflies would buzz and hover as the fish grew large and the turtles swam and the snakes all slithered down the bank there for a drink. One year, there was a very large snapping turtle, but I quickly got rid of him.

* * * * *

Autumn is Mother Nature brushing her hair.

* * * * *

Susan once told me that when we die God is going to pull back the curtain on our lives for us; He will show us everything we have ever done, and while doing so, He will reveal to us further how each choice led to the next, and how alternately our lives may have gone. I am starting to believe this may indeed be true.

The main thing I regret in life is that I have lived my life with regrets.

* * * * *

In autumn, there is always room for second chances…

* * * * *

I was administering Susan's morphine to her on a daily basis after it became too difficult for her to swallow the pills. Her neck was so thin it was hard to imagine even the tiniest of pills making it through there. She looked almost like a bird with bright blue eyes.

Sometimes she would hold her pen upon the paper for a very long while, and then, as inspiration took hold of her, she would manage a perfect sentence or two. Sometimes, as soon as she had punctuated the final line, her eyes would close swiftly and she would find herself in sleep.

During those pauses, I would examine her face from my chair, casually going over her eyebrows and her lashes, her small nose and her cutest little chin. Sometimes I would feel guilty, like some sort of voyeuristic vampire while doing this thing. However, when she would awaken to me and smile, and ask what I had been doing to keep myself busy after apologizing for having fallen asleep, I would tell her and she would ask me if she was still beautiful. To her question, I could most often only nod my affirmation, as it was almost too painful to speak my answer aloud.

* * * * *

Autumn is a time of letting go.

* * * * *

Sometimes the paper I brought for her remained covered in nothing but aimless, narcotic scribbles. I kept those pages too.

* * * * *

Winter is the perfect time to say, "I am sorry for letting you down."

* * * * *

When you hold the hand of a dying friend, it can sometimes feel as if you are an anchor; a weight upon the Earth connected to their soul by a thin silver line. They hold on as if that simple and gentle connection is the only thing keeping them from slipping away into eternity. Yet, they seem to hold on to your hand so loosely, as if to say you only have to do your job until it is time.

*   *   *   *   *

Autumn is the place where butterflies go when they slip into that slumber.

*   *   *   *   *

Susan was the most beautiful woman I think I was ever blessed to fix my eyes upon, and not just because she was pretty.

*   *   *   *   *

Winter is a dripping downspout wearing a skirt of ice.

*   *   *   *   *

They let me spend the night in Susan's room, which was something normally out of the question. I read to her from Leaves of Grass, and then I moved on to Keats and Shelley. She never slept as well as she did on those evenings when I read to her.

That night, I prayed for Susan's soul as I had never prayed before until I reached a point somewhere in the night when it felt as if God had touched my shoulder and told me everything was all right. Then I too fell asleep, and in the morning, I awoke to the first day of winter.

*   *   *   *   *

Winter is the time to admit that second chances are few.

* * * * *

The Lord took Susan from us on December 21st, the first day of winter, 1974. I discovered this fact at just about six am.

The light coming through the window of her room that morning was that dull, white light of winter, more of a glow than any light we more comfortingly know. I sat up straight and brushed my hair back with my fingers, and I could swear I felt something missing from that room.

Perhaps it is the absence of the sound of a person breathing that always gives us the first clue, or perhaps it is actually that we can sense that a spirit has died and a soul has left us.

I stood up knowingly. I stood up to stretch my aching back but it was only an excuse to avoid the inevitable. Then I arranged the poetry books from which I had been reading, on her nightstand, and then I moved closer to acknowledge the truth.

* * * * *

Winter is a time of thawing noses, rosy cheeks, and burning fingers.

* * * * *

I whispered her name twice, softly, and then I could feel my voice cracking and my heart inside my chest as it was slowly breaking before I could whisper Susan's name for the very last time. A nurse quietly walked into the room and cheerfully announced her good morning, but when I turned to face the door, her countenance fell like a stone.

I felt like a child wanting to ask this strange woman in the doorway just exactly what was happening then. After all, I would have done anything for just a few moments more alone with my love. The nurse-woman asked, "Is everything alright?" and all I could feel was my head swimming from the left and then to the right as the tears began to bubble up warmly from the geysers which had become my burning eyes.

219

If the skin of the face can curl or fracture, then mine curled like the wrinkled skin on a newborn puppy's back and fractured like an iceberg made of glass. I suddenly no longer knew what I should do then.

I wanted so hard to tell this woman Susan's story, to get her to fully understand whose passing presence she was in. I wanted to explain myself and all that we had been through. I wanted to die along with her, beside her.

I felt a need to remind this nurse that Susan had in fact fulfilled her purpose in life; how she had rescued a small child from the clutches of a predator. I wanted to remind everyone in that cold hospital that not everyone finds their purpose in life at all.

I wanted to force this woman to acknowledge that Susan Watts was the most incredible woman ever to have existed, and I wanted her to say those words aloud. I wanted to construct a monument to her with my feelings. I wanted to cradle her. I wanted to kiss her and to hold her. But then, but then I knew for sure I was on my own.

I felt my mouth open, but no words escaped me, and then I slowly turned back toward Susan's bed to where I could see her forever sleeping. Then suddenly I felt her mattress underneath my elbows, and then I felt my knees hit the cold, marble floor.

* * * * *

Winter is a time when things are done. Winter is a time of frozen aspects of the sun.

* * * * *

Susan could decorate a church for a party like no one I had ever met before. Unfortunately, due to the circumstances of her existence, and her choices, not a lot of other people appreciated her ways. The other women in town were so judgmental.

Susan was excellent with children. When she taught

220

children, she got down to their level, usually bending at the knees, but she never spoke condescendingly; she just offered what it was they had to know.

There were times when I would catch a glimpse of her after service on a Sunday, lovingly tying some child's shoe. In every move she made, you could see the desperation she felt in having not been a mother, yet she loved each one of them as if that child was her own.

Once I saw her sitting in a chair rocking with a crying child, rubbing the child's hair and speaking soothingly into its ear. When she made eye contact with me, she smiled as if to say she was experiencing the greatest feeling, and the utmost purpose in all the world.

* * * * *

Winter is a bluebird finally at rest.

* * * * *

Marvin Watts ended the lease on the house that he and Susan rented in town and he moved to the next town over in order to live out his life with Teesha Daniels and their child. I only saw him a few times after the funeral, and then it was if he had simply disappeared.

* * * * *

Winter is the Sabbath of the seasons.

* * * * *

The funeral was a small affair; Pastor officiated, his wife and I each said a few words. Not one of Susan's relatives attended, all for except her one cousin.

* * * * *

Winter is a blanket under which the future grows.

* * * * *

I held my own private ceremony back at my cottage with a bottle of very cheap booze and a fire. It was the first week of winter, and even though I was in mourning, the fires still needed stoked. By midnight, I had smashed the bottle into the fire of the furnace in the basement of the sanctuary. Later, I cried outside upon the wet and half-frozen ground, howling up at the Moon like the arc angel Michael with strands of Lucifer's hair between his fingers, with the damp of the earth beneath my knees seeping through my jeans.

* * * * *

Winter is a time for the remorseful and the young to come together to trade places through their stories.

* * * * *

I spent the next few days a wandering madman, avoiding the eyes of the public by staying out of view. I refused to shave. I would sit and read Susan's poetry. I would torture myself with recollections of her laughter as I dared recall the fact that I had thought of murdering Marvin at least a hundred times. I beat myself up in the mirror.

It all came to an end the hour Pastor knocked on the door to my cottage, carrying with him a porcelain urn filled with sweet Susan's ashes. He handed it to me as if it were a talisman designed for a greater purpose than merely containing some dusty remains. He handed it to me as if it were for me, as if she were mine.

Pastor reminded me that I had taken on the responsibility of spreading Susan's ashes. Then he blessed me and offered me kind words of hope, and then he was gone.

* * * * *

Winter holds a very personal and very private definition of

alone.

I sat with Susan's ashes in my small living room. Her urn was on my coffee table. I tried to pray and to contemplate what she would have me do. I tried to talk to her. I knew I was supposed to spread her ashes out over the pond, but what I did not know was when. Was I supposed to wait until the springtime? Was I supposed to wait until the flowers of summer were waving in the air? Had she hoped that I would remember that her favorite season was autumn, and live with her remains like a heartbroken widower, until the near end of the following year? I had no idea what to do with them. I no longer knew what she would say.

Winter can be a time of unexpected blessings.

Susan had always said that the only thing missing from the pond out back behind the church was a little rowboat. She had often asked me why I fished from the shore when it could have been so much more relaxing to sit lazily on a small wooden boat after rowing out towards the center, and then to simply let the breezes direct me where to go. She spoke of these things so whimsically and romantically that I would just sit and admire her outward gaze, as if I could see her actually seeing this small craft, as she sat with me on the shore.

"You could have a compartment to keep a cooler in with your lunch inside, and some iced tea on some ice and a few bottles of beer." She would laugh and add, "And you could have a bucket for your bait and another bucket for your fish, and when you were done fishing you could row your boat ashore while singing Hallelujah!"

Remembering her words brought me my first smile since the

223

moment she had died. At that moment, I stood up, brushed off my hands, and started to sketch my designs for a boat.

It was a simple little craft, nine feet long from bow to stern, and as you may imagine; there was an aft compartment, behind where I would sit, which contained enough room for a cooler, an anchor and rope, and some tackle and a net.

I set up sawhorses in the barn and worked on this boat in the cold. I oiled up all my tools and beat the rust from a few weathered hammers. I purchased copper nails, brass screws, and some marine plywood and oak from Barnett's hardware store. I drove into the city to purchase the cleats and the oarlocks.

For two months, I shaved the wood, drilled holes, tapped nails, and sanded down. Every night I did this thing by the light of two Coleman gas lanterns until my back was aching and my head and hands could not finish a task.

After completion of the frame, I stood and looked at this thing; this wooden frame that appeared more like a skeleton, like a huge oaken rib cage, and I felt as if I was in some way resurrecting Susan in bodily form by creating this boat.

During the month of February, I put the final finish on the body of the wood, sanding first with a rough grit, then working my way up to the finest. The smell of wood dust filled my senses perpetually, and the barn floor all around her was a blanket of shavings and yellow sawdust that only grew and grew.

I cried in that barn almost daily.

In March, I rubbed her entirety with linseed oil and I detailed every screw hole, copper nail, and wooden peg. Then I sanded her again and rubbed her with oil a second time. This process took a lot of patience, with a lot of time merely sitting as she dried. After filling the gas lanterns, I would sit, play with, and feed the feral cats that lived in the barn. I would examine her contours repeatedly, walking the length of her, and I would talk to both Susan and God aloud.

I did not have the heart to paint the boat any particular color, so instead I chose to stain her and then seal her with a lacquer finish. During late March and April, I cut a fine line with tape and I stained her underbelly dark walnut; her upper half and interior a tarnished forest gold like Susan's hair.

Two coats of linseed oil and two complete sandings, four coats of stain, and then fourteen layers of thin lacquer and her finish was complete. She would cut like glass upon the water.

Next was to purchase and hand-finish each of the oars to match her. I chose to finish each oar with the same tarnished gold, with a dark walnut stripe run straight through the half of each, where the handles meet with the oarlocks.

I made the tips of the blades dark too.

Come May, I left the boat in the barn and proceeded to refurbish the small dock at the near end of the pond. The dock was four feet wide and twelve feet long. When I was done with my work there, she was repaired, refinished, sturdy, and level. I then stained the dock planking too. I also added a cleat so I could tie up the boat there.

In the dark of the night, by lamplight, I would continue in my pursuit of the perfect name for this small wonder; a project inspired by Susan, the task that kept me from going insane. In the end, I chose to paint the word 'Autumn' in metallic gold lettering on the stern of the boat. The lettering was not perfect, but it was beautiful. I also added a tiny gold cross underneath.

I put her in the water to see if she would float on June 3, but as you may have guessed, I did not row her out until August 28th, 1975; the day Susan and I first met. Susan did not join me for the maiden voyage; I left her urn and ashes in my living room on the fire's mantle. This is where I kept her remains. No, I did not want to let her go quite yet. I waited until the first day of autumn, and it was on that day that I made that dreadfully lonesome walk down to the dock with her, alone.

* * * * *

Autumn is the perfect time to stop and think, *'There but for the grace of God, go I.'*

* * * * *

There is something about the feeling of stepping onto a small craft on the water. The experience provides both a sense of risk and a sense of security at the very same time. I you place your foot right, there is no reason to worry, yet taking that second step can often be the scariest step of them all.

I took that first awkward step with Susan's urn cradled in my arms on September 23, 1975; the first day of autumn. I would have fought the armies of Hell in order to hold onto her and not to let go of her until the appropriate time.

Just as Susan had always talked about, I packed a lunch, brought along two buckets, and even filled a cooler with ice and placed upon that ice a few bottles of beer. I put the beer inside the night before so it would be cold. My fishing pole was resting by my side.

Tying off from the cleat at the dock, I placed the oars into the oarlocks and then I pushed off from the dock and let her simply glide. It was a perfect first day of autumn. It was a day that tried to pretend it was still summertime.

I rowed slowly, smiling at Susan's urn and talking to her about the boat I had built in her memory; how it served to keep me from dying inside, and how I felt it was her final gift to me. As I had imagined while working all winter long; the smooth finish of the boat, along with her deep draft, allowed her to cut the water like glass.

The trip to the center of the pond only took a few minutes, and when I got to the center, I chose to do as Susan had always suggested, and I set no anchor, but decided to drift. There was no breeze to speak of, so there I remained, nearly perfectly still on that mirror-like altar of life.

It took all the strength I had to reach out for that urn after placing the oars down and setting them to rest within the boat. I thought about having a beer then, but then I decided to wait.

The sky was so blue it reminded me of Susan's eyes on the day I first met her, and I had to smile because there were only two clouds up above. Then I thought of my promise and I picked up the urn, but before doing anything with it, I looked up and asked God if Susan was in Heaven.

Just then, as I waited for my answer, a small golden leaf fell from the sky and listlessly remained after landing on the water. It was gold, more gold though than any yellow, and I had to stop and look around in order to imagine from where, or from which tree, or, despite the lack of any breeze, from whence this gift had come.

There was only one answer to that question…

Then I opened Susan's urn, reached deep inside most intimately and timidly, and began to spread her silken ashes upon the blessed waters with my trembling, and undeserving bare hands.

The end.

How Autumn Came to Be.

Autumn began as a seed planted in my heart by a waitress in Northern California in the summer of 1991. The diner she worked at was all but empty the morning I road my new mountain bike to its doors. The weather was grey and chilled. As I hungrily sat down at the counter, the rain began pouring down hard beyond the silvery frames of the windows. The rain had only been a light drizzle before.

Soon enough, a young waitress came in, shook off the weather, poured me a cup of black coffee, and then proceeded to tell me a story. Actually, it was less of a story than a series of complaints about her husband. According to her, he had refused to get out of bed to drive her to work in the rain. By the time I finished eating, I had watched and listened for over an hour as she desperately tried to rekindle her love and appreciation for her man. At one point, she had to walk away to cry.

For her tip that day, I had left her my brand new mountain bike so she would never have to walk to work again. Her story always remained with me.

Twelve years later, I was seated at a restaurant by the name of Nathan's Café in Enola, Pennsylvania. As I sat, mournfully nursing a beer, I asked God to bring me love. My short prayer was interrupted when a couple came in and sat down beside me. Upon casually acknowledging their presence, I was so struck by the woman's beauty that I had to get up and leave.

Why did I have to leave? I had to leave because what I felt was so powerful upon seeing her that I was afraid I might express my feelings to her, despite the fact that she was with another man. I had to leave because I felt that would have been wrong. I had to leave because I had never felt that way before, for any other woman on Earth, and in a way it frightened me.

The worst part of the experience was; as a poor, humbled writer, all I kept thinking was, "She is so fantastically beautiful, and even though she looks terribly unhappy with this man, she would never consider me." She was out of my reach, or so I imagined.

Five years later I began writing Autumn. I had gone through a

229

lot of heartbreak over those years and felt compelled to create something beautiful. So, I simply imagined a female character that served to combine all of my lost loves, and I created the rest of the setting and circumstances to fit the tale.

When I began writing this story, I was filling in as the cook at my church because the woman who previously held the job there had died. Every day I would see her apron in the pantry with her name tag affixed to it. This was her quiet memorial. Then after my shift was done in the kitchen, I would sit in the field next to the church, with pen and paper in hand. The prior cook, a woman I had never once met, had died of lung cancer…

One day, after cleaning up the dishes, a lovely blonde woman came in and asked if she could hang up some flyers on our bulletin board. As soon as I looked into her eyes, I recognized her as the woman from Nathan's Café five years earlier. My heart leapt in my chest beneath my apron. I felt like I was traveling through time. Her hair was long, and her eyes were blue, and she spoke as if her business was the most important thing in the world, and yet, she looked terribly unhappy.

I spoke with her briefly, alternatively gazing at her wedding ring, and then I sadly watched as she walked away. As inappropriate as this may sound; I felt my heart break as she left me. I had no idea how I could have remembered this woman after five long years, and yet I still felt the same way I had that first evening I saw her with her husband-to-be at the bar.

I felt more for her in those few minutes in my church's lobby than I had ever felt before in my life for any other woman; yet she was taken, never to be mine.

Two years later I walked into Nathan's Café with my brother. Instantly my eyes met with the eyes of a pretty blonde woman seated at the bar. Without a second thought, I left my brother's side and went to introduce myself to her. I looked at her hand. She wore no ring and our connection was instant.

Yes, it would turn out that she was the very same woman from Nathan's Café and from my church's lobby. However, I did not recognize her because she had cut off most of her hair and had lost a considerable amount of weight due to the stress of her impending divorce.

As the evening progressed, we talked, we danced, we sang and we laughed, and her girlfriends each told me that they had not seen her so happy in years. One of them even pulled me aside and said, "We all think you are a great influence on her. We haven't seen her smile in two years. You should definitely ask her out."

That night I told my brother he could leave me there at the bar. I just smiled and told him, "It's okay. I just met the woman I am going to spend the rest of my life with." He laughed and left me there.

You see, I was so captivated by her presence that I was willing to walk home in the cold just to stay by her side for a little while longer.

After a few days spent together socially, the two of us were swimming in our affections for each other. Everything felt right, almost magical. I was in love.

The strangest part of this story is; each time we had seen each other, I had just finished praying for love. The night I met her for the third time, I had just spent two hours praying for God to bring me my equal.

The details of Autumn, in fact, have nothing to do with her as I knew nothing about this beautiful woman when I penned it, and yet I truly believe it was my heartfelt want for her, a woman that I could not have, that inspired much of the story. Unfortunately, our meeting came about too soon after her separation and she was not yet ready to open up and trust another man. Despite my prayers, which seemed to have been answered that night, it would appear that fate did not hold a permanent place for us together, after all.

We spent many wonderful days and evenings together, walking in the woods and sitting by firelight talking well into the evening. She was broken when I found her, and we would often turn to one another to express how badly we both wished that we could have met each other at a better time. I did my best to lift her from her misery, but she was heartbroken and lost.

She told me that I was her angel...

Then it all fell apart.

I have not seen her since our last day together. I can only hope and pray that she is healing from her divorce, learning to be

231

happy, and finding her way back home. She was cocooned in her misery when I found her, and on that last day we spent together, she wore a shirt that featured a large butterfly on the back.

Autumn is a terribly tragic tale about loss and unrequited love. I hope it does as much for your heart as it has done for mine, for in many ways, I have lived this story many times over, again and again and again.

Made in the USA
Charleston, SC
29 March 2011